The Earth Stood Still

The Earth Stood Still
a novella

A novel by

Charles Lee Robinson Jr.

Casual Comfort Publication, LLC

USA / Florida

My Website: amazon.com/author/robinsonc

FOLLOW ME

Facebook: Charles Robinson

TikTok: @clrjr.1968

Instagram: jr.charlesleerobinson

Pinterest: crobinson1968

LinkedIn: Charles Robinson

Goodreads.com

Wattpad.com

Payhip.com

Readerslegacy.com

Tumblr.com

YouTube: https://youtu.be/6Ks3SQSHGw

...We were all minding our business...and then it came from nowhere...!

A Virus that was so deadly it shook our foundation. From that day forth our lives would never be the same. Many suffered and many died as our country faced an onslaught of deaths in just a little bit of time. People scrambled to sustain some normalcy. Heroes emerged and our survival tactics took over. We were in a war against an invisible enemy. Only God can save us!

PANDEMICA of 2020

The Earth Stood Still

2020

COVID STRAND 19

TABLE OF CONTENTS

Chapter 1

I Got my Big Promotion

{One}

{State of Colorado}

I remember running playing with my two children, my son Alex and my daughter Shicora and our dog Scruffy. We didn't have a care in the world. We were just playing and rolling all over the floor and then my Wife, Chancie came downstairs and she turned on the TV.

"Today, Stanley F. Pharmaceuticals said, they are looking for a few good Scientist from the U.S. to go over to China and assist with some experiments and hopefully, they can get some of the most intelligent Scientist from Stanley F. Pharmaceuticals and that's our news today, thank you, this is PGS news station, good night," The news anchor Ben Coglac said. Chancie turned and looked at me and said, "Did you hear that honey, this could be your big break," "Yes, I heard it, but I wouldn't want to leave you and the children," "Say what, ever since we graduated from college, you've been talking about being this Mad Scientist and getting that big promotion, yes, you better go,"

I turned and I looked at my children and said, "What do you guys think?" They jumped all over me and including Scruffy and they bellowed "go, go dad," Soon after, the phone rang and it was my supervisor at Stanley F. Pharmaceuticals, Mr. Saun Lee.

"Hello, hi Sir, sure yes, I can come in the office, I'll be there first thing in the morning," I said as I hung up the phone, a huge smile came across my face. Chancie ran over and gave me a hug.

"This is it, the reason you've been working so hard," she said. "So, you think of me as a Mad Scientist, do you?" "You know I am just playing with you about that, but no, Mr. Alexander M. Vector, and my dear husband, you are well qualified for the job,"

"Ha, ha, I was about to say, now come over here and let me show you what a Mad Scientist will do to you," Then I grabbed Chancie closer to me and started kissing and nibbling on her neck. She tried to keep me from kissing on her neck and then she said, "Honey not in front of the kids and we both started laughing as the children and Scruffy jumped all over us.

The children ate and they went to bed and Chancie and I headed to our bedroom. We both took our showers and I sat on my side of the bed, and as I was lying back on the bed, Chancie said delicately, “Come here my Mad Scientist, get over here,” We both started kissing and we finished the night off by making love.

The next morning my alarm went off and I was rushing to get to the office. I was running so fast; I forget my lunch on the kitchen table. I called Chancie and said, “Honey, I forgot my lunch on the table can you please put it up?” “Yes, I will but what will you eat?” “I’ll find something, I guess I’ll be alright though, at least I didn’t forget my coffee,” I said as I drank out of my coffee container.

Finally, I made it to the office and I could see so many people scrambling everywhere. A couple of my co-workers headed to Mr. Saun Lee’s office, Shareen Duvaye, and Sabian Daniels.

While everyone was still running wild in the office the three of us was called into a conference room with Mr. Saun Lee. Mr. Lee closed the door behind us and locked the door.

(Chinese/English accent) “Listen you guys and gal, you are my finest Scientist here at Stanley F. Pharmaceuticals, we have a top-secret experiment going on in my homeland China, and I want to be a

part of it, I am really counting on you to be a part of this, this is enormous to our company and also massive for your careers.

"Sir, I'm very enthusiastic, but what are you sending us to China to do?" Shareen asked with inquisitiveness. "Sir whatever it is, I am there, just tell me what you want us to do," Sabian said with his kiss ass attitude. "I am glad you asked and I am glad you have such a great attitude, now let me tell you exactly what you will be doing there,"

"I can't wait to hear this," I said. "Well that's a good thing Mr. Vector, because you will be the head of this operation and you will only take orders from me," he said as I stood inaudibly, but intrigued. Shareen started pacing with her arms crossed and Sabian stood as he held his pen and pad.

"Please, sit, sit, I want you all to listen and pay attention, because this will not only boost your careers but also take our company to new heights, again, this is top secrets and no-one can know the essence of what we are doing, not even the government of the United States of America can know, do you understand?" He asked with all seriousness.

"Mr. Lee, what is this top secret?" Shareen asked. "This sounds very somber, should I take notes Sir?" asked Sabian. Shareen and I both looked at Sabian and she rolled her eyes while I just grinned. "Please, carry on Mr. Lee, are attention is all yours," I said.

"Thank you, listen China is working on a wonder drug and it can cure any disease or virus known to man, I want us to be in on it, maybe we can win a Nobel Peace Prize when it's all said and done,"

"A wonder drug, let me write this down," Sabian said as he started writing in his pad. Shareen smiled and she shook her head.

"What kind of drug is this and why doesn't the government know about it?" I asked. "Again, like I said, its top secret, now can I count on you guys to lead for us, by the way Mr. Vector this is the big promotion you've been asking for," Mr. Lee said as he put both of his arms around his back and walked towards me.

"Wait a minute Sir, you're giving him a promotion, what about me?" Sabian asked with jealousy. "Don't you worry, I will take care of you also, is that understood?" Mr. Lee asked as he then walked towards the window. "Yes Sir, but just don't forget, I want a promotion also" Sabian said.

"Sabian, Sabian, relax, you will get your promotion and so will I, isn't that right, Mr. Lee?" Shareen asked with confidence.

"Like I said, you will all be compensated, now this mission will take you at least six months in China to assist top Scientists and some of the most intelligent Engineers the world has ever known, this mission will be led by Lui Pand and Mi Dem, they will be head of all experiments, but Mr. Vector you will be the head of this team, our team, is that understood?" I stood there in silence. I knew this was my big break, but damn, I have to be away from my wife and kids for six months. I put my hand over my mouth and paced back and forth as I thought about how Chancie and the kids wanted me to follow my dreams. Shareen walked over to me and she looked me square in my eyes and she shook her head up and down and I slowly nodded my head.

"I am all in Mr. Lee," Shareen said. "So am I Sir, hold up let me write this down," Sabian said. Shareen and I smiled and then we shook our heads at that kiss ass Sabian. "I'll do it, I will do it, so when do we leave," I asked. "Yes, yes, I knew it," Shareen said.

Sabian walked up to me and he whispered, "Now you know I am not going to listen to your ass, right," and he walked away while acting as if he was writing something in his pad. "By the way Sabian, if you don't listen to Mr. Vector, because he is in charge of this team, you will not receive your promotion," Mr. Lee said and that didn't sit well with Sabian. Shareen burst out giggling. I could tell Sabian didn't take to kindly to that but; oh well that's his business. This is not personal, it's all about successfully completing the project.

"Now when do we leave and when do we start?" Shareen asked.

"Next weekend, I'll get all you guys plane tickets and the place you will be staying at while you'll be over there, I'm sure Mr. Vector needs to run this by his wife and family," said Mr. Lee.

"Yes, I do, but I must say thank you for trusting me to help lead this company into the future with something as important as this, I do appreciate it and I won't let you down," I said with passion.

"Mr. Vector, I know you won't let me down, that's why I put my full trust in you,"

As we started walking out of the conference room, Mr. Lee put his hands around his back and walked over to the window and looked out of it; and then he looked back at us and nodded his head with a semi-smirk on his face. "Yes, yes, this is immense, this is enormous," Shareen said as we walked out the door.

"Sir," Sabian said. "Go Sabian, I will let you know more particulars later, now go and get your things together," Mr. Lee said. Sabian turned and he walked out of the door behind us.

I headed home to tell Chancie the good news, but I was stopped a few blocks before I was home by a road block made by the police. Others and I got out of our cars to see what was going on. Then we heard a yell and a scream from two Officers, "Get back get back in your cars," I was inquisitive so I didn't get in my car right away.

"Get in your car," the Officer ordered. I could see a Chinese man walking towards a short Officer with a machete. They were trying to get the man to put the machete down or they would be forced to shoot. The man didn't listen and he started charging the Officer with the machete. The Officer started running backwards and just before he fell in the middle of the street, he shot his gun twice, but missed. I immediately stooped backed into my car. Then I peeked over the dashboard and as soon as I did, the other Officer let out is K-9 and he charged the man; but the man swung the machete and beheaded the K-9. Afterwards all I heard after that was multiple gunshots and I hit the floor and I stayed there shaking and shivering. I started praying and hoping I didn't get hit with one of those bullets. I slowly lifted from the floor and looked over the dashboard and the man laid in the street motionless. He was dead. The Officer grab the body of his K-9 and yelled out a loud scream. It was a horrific sight.

When I got home, I was shaking and shivering. I walked in the house slowly. "Honey, are you alight, what's wrong?" Chancie asked as she hugged me firmly. I explicated to her what I just saw and she felt so badly for me. I just couldn't believe I witnessed a dog's head being chopped off and a man being shot dead in the middle of the damn street.

After Chancie comforted me, I ate dinner with her and the children and then I took a shower. When Chancie finished cleaning up the kitchen, she sat next to me and gave me a soft kiss and asked, "So how was your day, I mean beside that horrific ordeal you had to witness, did you get the promotion you've been looking for?"

"Oh yes honey, it almost slipped my mind because of you know what, but yes, I did," "Awesome, so tell me about it, when, where, tell me, tell me," "I hate to break this news to you honey," "What, what, tell me now,"

"Mr. Lee wants me to lead the team on a top-secret project,"

"Top secret, wow, so when?" I was hesitant at first, but I had to tell her. "He wants us to go to China," I looked up at her with an innocent look on my face. "Wow, China, okay, for how long?"

"He wants us over there for at least six months, now listen if you don't want me to go, I won't," "That's non-sense of course I want you to go and the children will be happy for you," "Are you sure, that is a long time I'll be away from you guys, and I will miss you all so much."

"You'd better go, I will not hold you back from your dreams, now of course, I will miss you, but we can skype and see each other every night," "I'm glad you understand, this is big for me, I want to make you and our children proud of me,"

"Honey, we are already proud of you, now go out there and do your best," "So, how top-secret is it?" "It's very top secret, but I can tell you this, not even the government knows about it," "Now that is classified for real honey, not even the government?" "Not even the government."

"Well, I hope it's not illegal," "Chancie, of course it's not, but I can tell you this, I will be working with a group of intelligent Engineers and Scientists over there in China,"

"How many of you are going?" "Only three from here, but I'm the lead Scientist in charge," "Who's going with you, do I know them?"

"You know Shareen?" "Yes, I like her, she's very keen," "And Sabian is the other, you remember him, right, I told you about him when Mr. Lee first hired him?" "You mean the one you said is a big ass kisser?" "Yes, that's him and you know what he had the nerve to whisper in my ear?" "What that honey?" she asked.

"He said he wasn't going to take any orders from me in not so many words," Really? So, I guess you have to show him who's in charge, huh?" Now, when are you leaving?" Chancie asked. "We are leaving next week," "Wow, so soon, well I guess you have a lot of love making to do," Chancie said as she grabbed me and pulled me on top of her.

Chapter 2

Making it to China

{Two}

{Wuhan, China}

Our plane landed in China and we were met by several Chinese men in business suits. They directed us to get into three different all black Bentley trucks. I found that kind of odd. ***Why didn't they just put us all in the same truck?*** As we drove for at least an hour or so, I noticed some Chinese people wearing masks. I thought maybe they were protecting themselves from pollution or something. Although I thought it was bizarre, I just shook my head and kept it to myself.

Finally, we made it to an enormous complex in a rural area called Pandemica Research Compound. The building was all white but its foundation and structure was outline in steel chrome. I noticed before the Chinese drivers of our trucks got out, they all put on masks and then passed each one of us a mask to put on. We put on our mask as our feet touched the soil. At the entrance of the complex stood two short Chinese men and one woman with masks on and they were wearing white Doctor Coats. Shareen, Sabian and I were reunited as we walked together towards the three of them. As we got closer, another short Chinese woman walked out of the electronic slide doors with a white clip board and she stood next to the others as she also wore a mask. We got closer to them and I observed they had red and white name tags with their names on them. The first one who bowed their head was Mr. Lui Pand and he didn't extend his hand at all to us.

"Hello, I am Mr. Lui Pand, welcome, we welcome you to Pandemica," His English was very fluent. The next one to bow their head was Miss *Mi* Dem. She was very soft spoken, but her accent was not as sharp in English, but I still understood her.

"Welcome, welcome," she said recurrently with several bows of her head. The other Chinese man spoke up also and he protracted his hand to all three of us, but he was wearing rubber or some kind of plastic gloves. His name tag read Tan Saki and in a smaller writing it read Pandemica Engineer.

"We are so glad you are hear, we have heard so much about your talents and they will be needed here at Pandemica, we thank you for coming, and standing next to me is my Personal Assistant Sue Ling,"

Mr. Tan Saki said as he pointed to the woman with the white clipboard.

"Come, come in now," Mr. Lui Pand instructed as he started walking into the compound. Sabian walked over to me and whispered in my ear, "These fucking people are strange don't you think?" "Sabian, stop being so disrespectful," I said with a crazed expression. "I am not, I'm just saying, they look like fucking stupid idiots," as Sabian continued talking to me. I just followed them, looked at Sabian and just shook my head. *Damn, he talks too much!* I thought to myself.

Mr. Lui Pand walked up to the door and he looked through a green lit pad. The door processed his eye as a passcode and then he had to turn a chrome key which sat in a large key hole, It sat above the green lit pad and then he put his right thumb in a curved, rubber pad that processed his thumbs pattern. The door opened slowly and we all walked in. We all followed Mr. Lui Pand as he explained to us what every room we passed was used for and these were some enormous science labs.

"This lab here is where we do a lot of our experiments on animals first," Mr. Lui Pand said. Sabian immediately walked over to the door and looked inside and then slowly moved back. Next, Shareen walked over and then she also, moved back slowly.

Finally, I looked in the room and I could see, rabbits, mice, dogs, cats, rats, and other domestic animals in cages and a few Scientists injecting some kind if serum in them with long sharp needles.

Then we got on a large crystal-clear elevator. Mr. Lui Pand had to use the same clearance he used for us to enter the building all over again in order for the elevator to move. He pressed the down button on the elevator and we had to go at least five floors underground. This facility was unquestionably a top-secret place. There were so many diverse labs all over the place and everyone looked like they were into their assignments. Mr. Lui Pand took us into a very large room with a very huge table. I guess this was their conference room. He asked us to sit at least six feet from each other, which I thought was odd. We were all asked to sit down on these hard white and chrome chairs as Mr. Lui Pand paced back and forth with his hands behind his back.

"Let us tell you why we are here, Miss *Mi* Dem, speak please," Mr. Lui Pand said.

"The reason you all have been summoned here is because we were searching for the best Scientists the world has to offer, in order for us to create a vaccine which may someday cure and save lives all over the world," "Mr. Vector, your work ethics and your brilliance in your field was heard to be impeccable and we are excited to have you assist in this groundbreaking project," Miss, *Mi* Dem delicately said.

“What type of vaccine are we looking to make and from whose standards?” Sabian asked with a bit of sarcasm. “I am glad you asked that question, Sabian, Sabian isn’t it?” Mr. Lui Pand asked. “Yes, so what’s your answer,” asked Sabian again. “Sabian, please be quiet,” Shareen said. “No, we should know if this vaccine we are supposed to be making is CDC or FDA assured,” Sabian said.

“To answer your question Sir, Mr. Sabian, yes, everything is all legal, I assure you this is the only way we operate,” Mr. Tan Saki said with a loud pitch in every word spoken.

“Excuse Sabiana’s tone Sir, we are here to help you anyway we can,” “We were sent here to help you and that’s what we are here to do, so where do we start?” asked Shareen. As we were conversing Miss Sue Ling was jotting down everything that was said. I’m sure of it because she kept starting and stopping as we were talking.

Then the door opened up and a Chinese man ran in and he was very animated. “Hello, hello,” the man said.

“Mr. Vector, Shareen, Sabian, this is one of our lead Scientists, his name is Mr. Wu Dung, he will be in charge when I am not around.”

“It’s a pleasure to meet you Mr. Wu,” I said. He just bowed his head and began talking to Mr. Lui Pand in their Chinese language. Then the conversation turned into a small debate or argument, because soon after they stopped talking, Mr. Wu Dang stormed out. Shareen,

Sabian, and I were confused. *What the hell just happened here? What did we miss here? We all stood speechless for minutes!*

"Never mind Mr. Wu, he's obviously under the weather, maybe even delirious, but that's another story, so now do you understand what we are expecting from you now?" Mr. Lui Pand asked.

"Yes, I guess, we are helping creating this super cure, so when do we start?" I asked. "We are looking for you to start by the end of the week, this Friday actually," Miss *Mi* Dem said. "Okay Friday it is dammit," Sabian said as he tried to shake Mr. Lui Pand's hand, but he was denied.

Shareen and I looked at Sabian and asked, "Why *would you do and say something so stupid? It's evident that he doesn't want us to be that close or near each other. Besides, since we've been here, he hasn't come close to us, nor has he shaken our hands when we arrived.*

"For now, we have reserved some hotel rooms for you guys in the city. I will take you back to the surface and back to the cars," said Mr. Tan Saki. We made our way back to the surface, with Mr. Tan Saki unlocking the elevator and the door for us to exit. Again, we all got into the same separate cars as before.

On our way to the hotels they were having us lodge in, I asked my driver, "Why is everyone wearing masks?" He didn't say a word, let alone even looked me in the face. So, I left it alone and just enjoyed the ride. I must admit I was surprised about so many Chinese people wearing them. Especially seeing them on my way to the hotel, they were everywhere. *What's going on in this damn country?* I thought to myself. We finally arrived at the same hotel, but we all had different rooms, which were conveniently located right next to one another.

Everyone in the hotel was wearing a mask, too. Then I stopped the Bellboy and asked him the same question I had asked the driver. "Excuse me, why is everyone wearing masks here?" I asked as I removed my mask. The Bellboy started ranting in the Chinese language and began pointing at my mask while making gestures to pull it up, so I did so speedily.

"What's wrong with these crazy ass fucking idiots?" Sabian said. Then another Chinese Bellboy walked up and he said, "Welcome, I am Ju Sin, what's the problem with your mask, Sir?" "We were just wondering why everyone is wearing a mask," Shareen said.

"There was a Malaria epidemic here and everyone got sick, so now we are all taking precautions as we wait for the Scientist to make a super cure, now that's all I can tell you, bye now and enjoy your stay," he respectfully said.

"I don't understand why they are so fucking secretive here," Sabian said. "I agree, damn, they don't want to tell you anything, anyways, I am hungry, what about you guys, let's eat," Shareen suggested. "I don't understand why all the secrets, but for now I will wear my mask, but okay, yes, let's eat, I am famished," I said.

After asking the hotel's front desk where we could go for food, they directed us to the outside market in town. We decided to at least give it a chance. The market was crammed with people. Lots of peddlers were out also. They were all trying to sell something. We just kept walking and looking at the Venders and all the food they were trying to sell. Nothing looked like American food.

A Chinese guy almost ran us over as he pulled up in front of us to talk to one of the store owners about buying some live rats. "Why is he buying live fucking rats?" Sabian asked. I shrugged my shoulders as I didn't know. "I hope he isn't going to eat those nasty damn things; hell, they were just as big as little fucking kittens," said Sabian.

Then we walked down some more and we saw a guy selling what looked like rats on a stick like a shish kebob. They looked like they were glazed with honey or something. Shareen started rubbing her stomach. "Are you okay Shareen?" I asked. "Hell no, just look at her, she looks like she's about to throw up, just as I am, damn, they are eating nasty ass rats," Sabian said.

"Now, I am getting sick, I'm not sure if I'm hungry anymore, yuck," said Shareen. As we walked further down, we saw cats and dogs being sold the same way. The craziest thing was, as we passed the area where this Chinese man was skinning a cat in front of his store, two Chinese guys began fighting over who would get the cat meat first. We couldn't believe our eyes. The police came over and took both of the guys to jail. We were now ready to get the hell out of dodge. Suddenly, I was not hungry anymore, and I don't think Shareen and Sabian were either. "Can we go now?" Shareen asked.

"So, what do you think about working with Mr. Lui Pand, Alexander?" Sabian asked me. "Yes, yes, we will head out, if I remember how to get out of here, but to your question Sabian, I am not sure what I think, but I know Mr. Lee trusts us to be here and to help them come up with this super cure," "Right, a damn super cure, which is bullshit," Sabian said with sarcasm.

"Are you always this negative Sabian, you know what; don't answer that, you kiss ass," Shareen said. "Kiss ass, who's a kiss ass, you're not talking to me, that must be you, you're a kiss ass," Sabian said. "People stop it, let's not fall apart here and start calling each other names," I said. "Alexander, you know he's a kiss ass," said Shareen. "I am not, you are," Sabian said like a little child.

"People stop it, hey look, isn't that Mr. Wu down there buying something?" "Where, oh, it does look like him," said Sabian. "I wonder what he's doing here," Shareen said. "Let's catch up to him, maybe he'll tell us why he stormed out and was angry with Mr. Lui Pand," I said. We started walking faster so we could catch up to Mr. Wu. As soon as we got near him, he grabbed a bag from the guy who was selling him something and started walking away, so I decided to yell out his name.

"Mr. Wu, hello," I said, deafeningly. Mr. Wu turned around and saw who I was, and immediately started running away, and I mean, he was running fast. We jogged up to where he had retrieved his bag, and what I saw was stunning. "Why did he run?" Shareen asked. "I don't know, but look," I said. "What the hell, why was he buying fucking fried bats?" Sabian asked. "Damn, that's disgusting," said Shareen.

"Excuse me, Sir, are those really bats?" I asked. The guy smiled, and his teeth were brown, even though I was wearing my mask; his breath smelled fishy or something equally unappetizing. He spoke in Chinese, so we couldn't really comprehend him. A Chinese boy walked up to us, and he looked at me and said, "Sir, please do not eat the bats, they are poisoned with rabies, and some say they have a virus. I think I heard my older brother say it is called COVID, therefore do not eat it, it will kill you."

"How do you know this, who is your brother and why would people buy it if they know it will make them sick or like you say, kill them?" "I just told you what my brother told me, it is true, but you do not have to listen to a little child, go ahead and eat it at your own free will." The Chinese boy said. "Boy, what's your name?" Sabian asked.

"I am Wey, that is what they call me," "Thank you for warning us, Wey, but we weren't about to buy anything, we just saw somebody we knew over here buying these…damn bats," I said.

"Be careful, because people who buy the bats eat them and they can pass sickness or they can make poison which can cause a deadly effect to everyone," he said. "Thank you, Wey. I may need your help soon. We appreciate the information," I said. *Why was Mr. Wu buying bats?*

Chapter 3

Experimenting

{Three}

{On Skype with Mr. Lee}

"Mr. Vector, how is everything going?" "Mr. Lee, everything is satisfactory so far, but I must say, some bizarre events are occurring here." "Bizarre, what do you mean? Have you guys started experimenting and working with Mr. Lui Pand?"

"Actually, we are starting to work tomorrow, as far as bizarre, everyone here is wearing a mask and I do mean everyone, even here in the hospital." "I am sure that's procedure, because of an outbreak they had there recently." "So, you knew about an outbreak, Sir, why didn't you tell us?" "You didn't need to know that; besides, one reason you are there to help find a cure, a cure that will cure all."

"You may not think we didn't need to know that, but I beg to differ, we all have families, and I believe out of respect, you should have given us a heads up, Mr. Lee." "Are you questioning me? Look, I sent you there to help the scientists and Engineers find a cure. Now, if you don't want the promotion or the job is too challenging for you, let me know," he said in a nasty tone.

Before I spoke, I had to think about it because at that moment I was pissed off. I took a breather, and then I said. "No, we can handle it. I just wish you had warned us. We will help find the cure. Thank you for this opportunity. I will keep you posted on what's going on with the experiments."

"Thank you, Mr. Vector. I am glad you see things my way. I will check on your colleagues and contact you next weekend. Please make us proud, which I am sure you will. Bye, Mr. Lee." I said with an attitude. *That son of a bitch!* I said as I disconnected my Skype.

After speaking with Mr. Lee, I decided to call my wife, Chancie, and my children on the phone. I wanted to tell her what was going on over here, but I didn't want to alarm my family, so they wouldn't worry about me while I was here. I reassured her that everything was going well, and I missed them; then we hung up the phone. Shareen called me on the hotel phone, and she wanted to talk, so I told her to meet me in the hotel lobby. I forgot to put on my mask, and I was immediately stopped by hotel security and sent back to my room to retrieve it. They were very adamant about my getting my mask and putting it on. Shareen saw me on the way back to my room.

"Mr. Vector, what's wrong?" Shareen asked. "They made me come back to the room to get my mask, damn, they are serious about this, something isn't right here, you got yours?" "Hold up, oh no, let me get mine also, wow, are they taking extra precautions, like that?" "Taking precautions is an understatement; they acted like they wanted to call the police and arrest me or something." Shareen went and retrieved her mask, and we went downstairs into the lobby.

"Did Mr. Lee contact you also?" I asked. "Yeah, I talked to him and I didn't like how he was talking to me, I pretended the connection was bad and hung up on him while on Skype," "Ha, ha you did what, well good for you, I thought it was me, he was acting a bit mean to me, even when I told him about everyone wearing mask."

"I asked him why they were wearing masks, and I didn't like his answer, but after I hung up on him, I got on my computer so I could educate myself about what's going on here." "So what did you come up with?"

"China was nearly wiped out by the virus called Ebola, and then lately Malaria, it got so bad they couldn't give people real funerals, they just threw them in a field, and some were even burned to ashes."

"You mean they were cremated?" "Yes, that's actually what I'm saying, after thousands died, they started slowly coming back to some kind of normalcy."

"That's crazy, I wish we were informed before coming here, but now we are here, and we must find a cure," Shareen said. "Well, if we want to be in good health, we need to wear these masks and be safe and protected," Shareen said.

As we were conversing, Sabian walked by us. He didn't see us, and I was about to call out to him, but then I noticed him walking up to an unknown Chinese man. He handed him something, and then he walked back to his room, I suppose.

"What was that about?" Shareen asked. "I don't know, but we must keep our eyes and ears open," "Definitely, Mr. Vector, well let me get to my room and do some more research, I'll meet you down here tomorrow as we head to the compound to work on this cure," "Okay, that's a good idea, good night Shareen," "Good night," Shareen said and we both walked to our rooms.

Most of the night I couldn't sleep. I pulled my chair to the window and looked out for hours just thinking. I finally fell asleep around 3 a.m.

I awoke about 6 a.m. that morning due to a loud knock at the door. I looked through the peephole, and it was the driver that Mr. Lui Pand had sent to pick us up. They were at all of our doors at the same time, so we had to hurry to get dressed. While we were en route to the compound, I tried to speak with the driver once again.

"Excuse me, why do we have to be here so early?" I asked, and again he was absolutely quiet. "Do you talk, can you speak English?" Again, he said nothing. I just sat back and shook my head.

We arrived at the compound, and Mr. Lui met us at the entrance. He led us to a large laboratory, where he assigned each of us a designated area to work. There were many animals in there, and they were caged up for testing. We immediately got to work. I worked diligently on my computer, trying to come up with a cure. Occasionally, we would converse and come up with various formulas and techniques.

"Listen, while you and Sabian work, I'm going to use the restroom. I think we passed it when coming here." I said as I walked out of the lab. "Okay, we got this, Mr. Vector," Shareen told me as I was already in the hallway. I walked down a long hall and passed about five labs until I came upon one where I saw Mr. Wu working. He was moving in and out around a white curtain. He was fully protected in gear and dressed in white from head to toe, which looked anomalous.

I watched him for a little while. Suddenly, I saw a human foot fall to the side of what I believe was a bed. Mr. Wu had a large needle in his hand. I rubbed my eyes to make sure I wasn't seeing anything false. He didn't notice I was at the door watching him.

I couldn't tell if the person was dead or just on anesthesia. I wasn't told they were testing on people. *What the hell is going on here?* I thought to myself. I was just about to sneak in until I felt a hand on my shoulder. "Mr. Vector, may I help you with something?" Mr. Tan Saki said as I jumped from being startled.

"Oh, I'm sorry, I thought this was the restroom." I quickly answered. "I am sure you did, come here the restroom is down this way." he said. Just as I was going to walk away and follow him, I could see Mr. Wu pull something out of his pocket and stick a needle in it. I couldn't see what the object was, but I knew Mr. Tan Saki was standing right there and I had to hurry before he got suspicious.

I used the restroom and when I finished, Mr. Tan was waiting on me so he could escort me back to the lab. Except he didn't take me back the same way we came. We must have gone around another way because I didn't see the lab where Mr. Wu was working with that body. *I wondered if the body were still alive.* Unfortunately, that's all I could do was wonder. Mr. Tan Saki led me right back to the lab. I slowly walked in.

"Mr. Vector, what took you so long, never mind come over here and see what Sabian and I have found under the microscope," Shareen said. I ran over to see what they found. 'While you were gone Mr. Lui

Pand came in here with some sick rats, see there they go over there," said Shareen anxiously.

"Where did you go anyway?" Sabian asked. "I went to the restroom, why?" I asked. "I just asked because Mr. Lui Pand didn't seem really happy that you weren't here working on this with us and you're supposed to be our leader," Sabian said with cynicism.

"Never mind Sabian's questioning, Mr. Vector, look at this, we have a rat who was sick here and he somehow recovered, now this one is sick, I took the plasma from the rat that was healed and I injected his plasm in the sick rat, he seems to be doing a little better, but we have to give it some time," Shareen said.

"Who are you talking to, saying never mind to me, I don't think so," Sabian said with an attitude. "Sabian, do you ever shut the hell up sometimes?" I asked. Sabian was surprised when I said that. He became very quiet and walked over to his computer, looking dismayed.

"So how did you come up with this inkling, Shareen?" I asked. "Well, actually, Sabian and I came up with it together," answered Shareen. Sabian just looked over towards us, and he reluctantly walked back over to where we were working.

"Hey, there's something I need to tell both of you while I was on my way to the restroom," I whispered. "What's that, Mr. Vector?" asked Shareen. "What happened, tell us now," Sabian insisted.

"Hold your horses, let me make sure no one is coming down the hall," I said as I went over to the door and looked down the hall to ensure no one was approaching, then I put my head back in the room.

"Listen, I saw Mr. Wu working in a lab down near the restroom," "So, what the hell does that mean?" asked Sabian with his smart-ass mouth, "I think he was using a person for testing," "Again, what the hell does that mean, this is a lab," said Sabian.

"Do you want to hear this or not, I know he's supposed to be working on animals, but not humans and besides, this person didn't appear to be alive, I mean I couldn't tell," "The person was dead, is that what you're telling us?" Shareen asked with her eyes wide open.

"I saw a foot fall limp as I was watching him go in and out of the white curtains. I couldn't see the person's face, and as soon as I was going to walk in, I got caught by Mr. Tan Saki."

"So, you couldn't confirm if the body was alive or not?" Sabian asked. "No, I couldn't, I also noticed Mr. Wu injected the body with a needle and a huge needle at that." "I wonder what he was doing, come on, let's go see with our own eyes," Shareen said."

"I am not going, you too go, and I'm going to stay right here," Sabian said. "Fine, stay here, come on, Mr. Vector, let's go," Shareen said. Shareen and I left the lab to investigate on our own. We walked down the hall, but couldn't find anything. Mr. Wu wasn't there nor the body. I know my eyes weren't playing tricks on me.

“Mr. Vector, are you sure you saw him?” asked Shareen. “Yes, I am sure, now let’s go inside.” I said as we entered the lab where I believed I saw Mr. Wu. Shareen and I walked in and we started searching for things on the computers and some notes were laying on the cabinet, we searched through them all as well.

“Are you sure you saw him in here Mr. Vector, it doesn’t look like anyone has been in here for a while.” “Look at this, these notes say differently.” I said as I passed her some notes that were dated for today. Shareen eyes got big and then I noticed something under the table. “Shareen look, what’s this?” I asked as I picked up a brownish-black object. “What is it?” “Oh my God, it’s the wing of a bat,” I said while in shock.

“Why is it in here?” “I don’t know, I do remember seeing Mr. Wu pulling something out of his pocket and inject a needle in something, but I couldn’t verify because Mr. Tan Saki caught me as I was watching.” “Oh my God, what is going on here?” “Shareen, I really don’t know, but I’m telling you I saw a body in here,” Then suddenly we heard a noise and we ducked down and hid. Someone entered the lab and we stayed quiet.

“Mr. Vector are you in here?” I heard Sabian’s voice ask. “Yes, I’m here, I thought you were staying put,” I said. “I was, but I got a little curious too.” “Let’s get out of here before we get caught,” Shareen suggested.

"What did you find, did you see a body?" Sabian asked while being funny. "No, we didn't, but I'm with Shareen, let's get out of here." I said as I tucked the bat wing inside my pocket. Shareen saw me and while Sabian wasn't looking, she gave me a gesture as to not say anything, and I stayed quiet.

I peeped out of the lab door and made sure the coast was clear, then we walked out and headed towards our lab. As soon as we made it to the door and walked in, Mr. Lui Pand and *Mi* Dem were waiting for us. We all were looking like deer in head lights and my heart was pumping very hard. *Damn, I hope we're not in any trouble!*

Chapter 4

Day one of the spread

{Four}

We didn't get in any trouble because we made up a lie that we were all using the restrooms. Mr. Lee and *Mi* Dem then said they checked the restrooms. Then we explained to them we just took a little walk to stretch and then we got lost. I think they believed us because we went right back to working until our work day was completed.

Later on, that evening, I got on my computer and decided to do some research about bats, every domestic animal the Chinese have eaten, and to research the latest viruses and the potential cures they had in place.

I discovered some information that was intriguing and I called Shareen and asked her to meet me in the lobby. She said she had found some valuable information as well.

We both met down in the hotel lobby with mask intact on our faces. “Hey Mr. Vector, look at this, check this out,” “Okay, what did you find?” “Look at this article, it says here the Chinese have been reporting they have these viruses under control, but here it states thousands of people have been missing, and suddenly, bodies have been missing from the hospitals after autopsies revealed they had a virus,”

“Wow, now if that is the case, they have been lying to the United States about this, but why, millions of people can die.” “I’m not sure why, maybe they don’t want to disclose this information to keep the population down here,”

“Do you mean kill their own people, but for what gain?” “Maybe for money issues, I don’t know, right now they are the second richest country and the United States is the third,” “Who’s the richest country?” asked Shareen. “It says right here France is the richest country.”

“But why kill their own people, that doesn’t make any sense.” “Maybe the whole country isn’t in charge, but somebody is, we really need to find this super cure before the whole world is at stake, so what did you come up with, Mr. Vector?”

"Well, I discovered all these domestic animals they've been consuming here is the reason they've been having so many outbreaks, this country has been having so many ailments for centuries." "Yes, I could see that, remember all those animals at the market that day, it's crazy."

"Another thing, most of the owners in the market know the meat isn't safe and they still sell it and the customers still eat it, and regarding the bats, they carry lethal diseases and rabies, I also believe someone is making some kind of chemical warfare to wipe mankind off the earth."

"Don't you think your stretching it a bit?" "I really do hope so, otherwise, why was Mr. Wu buying bats and why was there a piece of bat wing in the lab?" "Do you think Mr. Wu has something to do with this?" "I am not sure; we have to do some more investigating?"

As we were going over what we both found, Sabian walked by us and again, he met up with the same Chinese man we saw before, and handed him some papers. "Did you see that?" Shareen asked. "What is Sabian up too, oh shit, maybe he's a spy or something," I said. "A spy for who, the United States, or do you think he's a Benedict Arnold?"

"He must be engaging in espionage or something." "We must keep what we know amongst you and me," said Shareen. "Maybe we should tell Mr. Lee about what's going on, what do you think?" "I don't think we should until we have more evidence of what's going on." "Maybe you're right, I won't say a thing, at least not just yet," Sabian walked back by us, and he didn't look our way. Whatever he's involved in, it's serious!

"Shareen, please email me all of what you've found then I can save everything we know on a secret flash drive on my computer, we need to save all the data we find." "I will definitely do that, and if I find anything new, I'll direct those emails to you as well."

Shareen and I talked some more, and we vowed to find out as much as we could. I knew we had to be careful because this country would arrest us for even looking suspicious about anything.

When I returned to my room, I retrieved all the information from Shareen's email and added what I had discovered. I then placed it in a top-secret zip folder and sent it to my home computer in the United States. I called my wife Chancie and told her what I'd done, but I didn't tell her about all that was going on. A part of me wanted to say something to her, but I didn't want to scare her, so I decided to tell her when the time was right.

The next day, back at the lab, we were still searching for a super cure. We noticed that certain developments from using the blood plasma from the rats were somewhat effective, and we decided to inject some blood plasma into cats.

For some reason, the cat's symptoms got worse, and some reacted inversely and died. I decided to go back to the drawing board because something was missing. Then a thought crossed my mind.

"Shareen, I remember reading about a drug that India used to control Malaria. Perhaps if we mix that with the blood plasma, we will see more positive results." "That's an exceptional idea, but where will we get some from?" "I know that's the problem, but I'll work on that."

Suddenly, the door to the lab opened, and it was Mr. Lui Pand. He instructed us to meet in the conference room. When we arrived at the conference room, Mr. Lui Pand started asking us questions about our research.

"It's been a couple weeks now, what are your findings thus far, what have we come up with for the cure?" He asked. Shareen and I looked at each other. We knew we had to tell him something. "So far, we've determined that blood plasma works regarding keeping the virus under control, but certain animals react differently, though," I said.

"So, what is missing Mr. Vector, you are an intelligent man, I am sure you know something by now," Mr. Lui Pand said as the tone of his voice got gaudier. "Uhm, we just need more time to study the development of different animals, and then eventually we'll need a live host," Shareen said as she interrupted Mr. Lui's aim at me.

"Are you saying you need live humans?" Mr. Lui asked. "Yes, that's exactly what she's saying, I know you have some people who may want to volunteer, right?" I asked. "Mr. Lui, we are very close to a cure, Sir, as my colleagues said, we just need human subjects," Sabian said. Shareen and I looked at each other, surprised that Sabian had spoken up.

"First of all, Mr. Vector, we have never, ever experimented on humans here at any of our labs," said Mr. Lui. At that point, I was bewildered, because I was sure that I saw Mr. Wu injecting something into a lifeless body in one of the labs in this compound. Right after that comment, Mr. Tan Saki walked in.

"Mr. Tan Saki, do you have anything to add here?" Mr. Lui asked. "As a matter of fact, I do, we are now getting all of our machinery together to be equipped to create thousands of tiny tubes to store the vaccine in, and in a matter of weeks, we will be able to produce millions, so all we are waiting on is the cure," Mr. Tan Saki said.

"Thank you, Mr. Tan Saki, Mr. Vector and his team are still working on the cure, and from what I hear, it should be soon, isn't that right, Mr. Vector?" "Like I said…" But before I could finish my reply, Mr. Lui interrupted me. "Thank you, Mr. Vector." Mr. Lui Pand said as he interrupted me, dead in the middle of a sentence.

"Okay, we will be waiting, Mr. Vector." Said Mr. Lui Pand, "I will now excuse myself." Mr. Tan Saki said as he turned around and left the room. Then, crashing in through the door was Mr. Wu, holding

Sue Ling, Mr. Tan Saki's assistant. "What is this, what's wrong with her Mr. Wu?" Mr. Lui Pand asked.

"She's sick, she needs a cure, now." He said angrily. Mr. Lui started walking near her and Mr. Wu. "Stay back dammit, she's sick, she needs a cure, I will find it myself." Mr. Wu ranted on and on.

"Let us save her, Mr. Wu," Shareen screamed. "Save yourself, no one wanted you Americans here anyway, we can find our own cure, now get the fuck out of here now," Mr. Wu yelled.

"Mr. Wu stop this madness now, she needs medical assistance, just look at her," Mr. Lui Pand said as Sue Ling body looked lifeless. Then I thought to myself, maybe she was the body I saw in Mr. Wu's lab, perhaps he injected her with a virus.

"We need to get her to a hospital before she dies, Mr. Wu, please let her go now," said Sabian. "You shut your mouth, American. I should have injected you, Mr. Lui. I told you we did not need these Americans to help, and you went behind my back and sent for them anyway, we are the supreme country, not them, damn Americans."

"Mr. Wu, please put her down, so we can take care of her and possibly save her life," I begged. "Do not get close to me, now, Mr. Lui, you lied and I trusted you, now you must pay, and so will your American friends." Mr. Wu said.

"What do you plan on doing?" Mr. Lui Pand asked. Then the lab door opened, and it was *Mi* Dem. She started screaming and begging Mr. Wu to let Sue Ling go as well. He wouldn't listen. He just kept ranting about destroying the United States and taking Mr. Lui Pand down with us.

"You are a traitor, Mr. Lui, you are a traitor to your country, and you will pay. I promise you, I will unleash this virus upon all mankind." Mr. Wu spoke in a mix of English and Chinese.

While Sue Ling dangled from his arms, he ranted on and on, and as soon as Mr. Lui Pand thought he saw an opening, he started running towards Mr. Wu at full speed. Then as he reached at Mr. Wu's neck, he stopped dead in his tracks, as he looked downward, he felt a piercing sting to his abdomen. Mr. Wu had pulled out a long needle that contained the virus and stuck him with it. He then dropped Sue Ling to the floor like a ton of bricks.

"Mr. Lui, no Mr. Lui," *Mi* Dem yelled out. "I told you that you would pay, didn't I, and now you will die, you and Sue Ling, unless you're stupid American friends find the cure," said Mr. Wu, and then he bolted out of the compound as Mr. Lui Pand lay there, clinching his abdomen.

"Check her, is she okay?" I asked. "I'll check, let me see," Sabian said. "Mr. Lui, are you okay?" Shareen asked. "Where is Mr. Tan Saki?" I asked. "I don't know, but we need to call the authorities now and get these two off to the hospital," Shareen said. "I'm on it now," Sabian said as he made a call to the authorities.

"Somebody needs to stop that crazy man," I said. "They will, now it's inevitable that we must find a cure." Said Shareen.

"Does she have a pulse?" I asked, and Sabian started checking Sue Ling's pulse. "It's very weak, I called the authorities, they'll be here shortly, are you okay Mr. Lui Pand?" Sabian asked. I believe Mr. Lui Pand was in shock because he spoke softly, "I will be okay, thank you; we must find that mad man and he must pay for his treachery."

"Yes, he will pay Mr. Lui," *Mi* Dem said as she took off her mask and comforted him. Finally, the ambulance and the authorities came and took Mr. Lui and Sue Ling to the hospital.

We made it to the hospital, and they took Mr. Lui Pand and Sue Ling into their own rooms. Sue Ling was put on a ventilator, and she was in really bad shape. We sat in the Lobby waiting to hear some news, and then *Mi* Dem started coughing profusely.

"*Mi* Dem, are you okay?" I asked. She was just coughing and coughing, and she almost choked. "Are you okay, hey, what's wrong, she may have to be examined while we're here," Shareen said. "No…no…I…am. Okay, okay." She said, and then she passed out.

"She might be infected also, get her some help," I said. Sabian told the Doctors, and they came and took Sue Ling back to get a proper diagnosis. Then out of nowhere, Mr. Tan Saki ran in asking questions, but where the hell has *he been all this damn time? We just ignored him, but we also knew he was the next in charge after Mr. Lui Pand.* Because of Mr. Wu's cowardly acts, this was day one of the spread!

Chapter 5

People are getting sick

{Five}

{The Pandemic Has Begun}

Sue Ling was so sick; the Doctors immediately put her in ICU on a ventilator. Mr. Lui Pand had to go in quarantine for at least fourteen days. The hospital Doctors said we couldn't have any contact with them.

A few days later Sue Ling died of complications from her lungs. We were all saddened. We continued researching for a cure day and night under Mr. Tan Saki's guidance. Every now and again, we checked in with Mr. Lee until his condition turned worse within a week. Eventually, they had to put him on a ventilator.

I sat in the lab and studied the dynamics of genetics and other components; just trying to figure out what type of strain was this virus creating. Shareen, Sabian, and I couldn't get any sleep.

While Shareen worked on different drugs, which had the same effects as the drugs India used for the virus that hit in the past, Sabian studied some specimens under the microscope. After coming up empty, Shareen walked over to me. She looked very exhausted.

"Mr. Vector, we're going to need to get our hands on that drug called Hydroxychloroquine, it is our only hope, and you must get in contact with Mr. Lee back home." Sabian put his hand on his chin and said, "She's right, we aren't getting any damn where, and there are far too many lives are at stake." I looked at both of their faces and I could see they were both exhausted, because of their bloodshot red eyes. I agreed to call Mr. Lee, but soon after; Mr. Tan Saki ran into the lab and he was breathing very worryingly.

"Come, we must go down to the hospital, they are saying *Mi* Dem is now in critical condition, she might not make it." Mr. Tan Saki said in a miserable tone. We made our way to the hospital and the scene was much different than the way we left the last time. Everywhere you looked there were people coughing and sneezing. It's a good thing each one of us was wearing our masks, because the people in the hospital looked like there was something very contagious going around. The area where Mr. Lui Pand, Sue Ling, and *Mi* Dem were very isolated rooms away from everyone. There were lots of people with protected gear on there. Some people wore masks and gowns and others didn't. Most of the people who weren't wearing them were coughing and sneezing severely.

'What's going on here, everybody seems so damn sick." Sabian said. "It sure seems that way." Shareen said as an elder lady walked by her and she sneezed right by an older man who was not wearing a mask. The man sat down in a chair with a nurse to get his vitals checked. We kept walking until we made our way to where Mr. Lui's room was located. The nurse insisted we wore these white protected gowns and a plastic shield over our faces along with our masks, along with white shoe coverings made of the same material as the white gowns were. The whole area was heavily taped up. The walls were taped up with a very thick plastic with yellow caution tape everywhere. It felt like we were entering a square plastic chamber or something. It felt peculiar and it was eerie.

"I hope Mr. Lui Pand is alright." I said as I sounded muffled wearing all the protected gear. "He is down here, two rooms on the right." a nurse said as she walked right pass the three of us. "How is he doing?" Shareen asked the nurse. "Here he is, unfortunately he is in bad shape, but the doctors are being optimistic." Said the nurse.

"Excuse me mam, what's your name?" Sabian asked as the nurse checked Mr. Lui Pand's chart, and she was also wearing protected gear including some white plastic-rubber like gloves. "Who me, I am Kim." she answered as she looked through Mr. Lui Pand's charts some more, and then she pressed a couple of buttons on his ventilator.

"How is he, will he live?" Shareen asked. "Look at him with all those tubes in his mouth." I said. "He can't breathe without a ventilator?" A faded voice said, and it was that of Mr. Tan Saki's." "Where did you come from, I didn't know you were coming back here, you just reappear like you're a ghost or something, you nearly scared me to fucking death." Said Sabian.

"I am everywhere" Mr. Tan Saki said as he was also dressed in all-white protective gear. "I didn't know you were coming back here." I said to Mr. Tan Saki. But he didn't answer back.

"To answer your question Sir, his lungs have been affected and he cannot breathe without the ventilator." said Kim. "Does he have an upper respiratory infection as well?" I asked. "Yes, he does, we must keep a close eye on him and we must continually check his vitals."

Then suddenly some kind of beeping noise down the hall started going code red. Someone in the hospital was flat lining. Kim ran out to see where the noise was coming from and we followed behind her. She met up with Doctors in front of Sue Ling's room. The Doctors were trying to save her, but unfortunately, she died right there.

Everyone was in protected gear with the exception of one nurse, who walked up after Sue Ling died and she suddenly started coughing; and I mean she was coughing copiously. Kim and a couple of doctors immediately escorted her out. With tears running down her face Shareen looked at me and said. "Mr. Vector we have to find a cure."

"Did you see how fast that nurse started coughing?" Sabian asked. "I am going in the back to check on Mr. Lui Pand, Mr. Tan Saki said with very little emotion. "I'll call Mr. Lee on Skype when we get back to the hotel later, and I wonder if the authorities have caught Mr. Wu." I said. "They definitely need to catch that asshole; he might spread this deadly virus everywhere fucking he goes," said Sabian.

"I can't take any more of this today, can we please go; this is getting out of hand, how can we stop this virus; questioned Shareen in an irritated demeanor. When we got back to the hotel, I called Mr. Lee on Skype but he didn't answer immediately. I pulled out my computer and started doing some more research.

Then, I noticed in the news tab, people were dying from a virus. I clicked on the tab and they started talking about the hospital in which Mr. Lui and *Mi* Dem were admitted. The news reported a dozen workers were infected and sick. After reading a little more, I stopped as I was interrupted by a Skype call from Mr. Lee. I updated him in on everything that was going on and he couldn't believe it.

"Oh no, I want you guys back to the United States," insisted Mr. Lee. "We can't come back now Mr. Lee; there are too many people lives at stake, we must find a cure." "Okay, I will give you a little bit more time to develop a cure, but not much, because if what you are saying is true, this virus can spread to other countries and kill more innocent people."

"I never looked at it like that Mr. Lee, but I suspect this virus has been here for a long time, because people were wearing masks prior to our arrival and they even had all three of us ride in three separate cars, which I thought that was very peculiar."

"Yes, China is my country and for centuries, I have heard of us fighting Pandemics and different viruses and based on what you are saying; this one sounds very contagious, even worse than the others," Mr. Lee said with a sound of concern. "This one is deadly Sir; I've seen what it can do in just a matter of weeks,"

"I am only giving you guys a few more weeks in China with a cure or not, then you all are coming back to the United States, and continue to keep me updated on what is going on with Mr. Lui Pand, and *Mi* Dem." "Okay Mr. Lee, I'll keep you posted and I'd like to thank you for giving us a little more time, oh, I almost forgot, if you can, we need to have access to a drug called Hydroxychloroquine, which is what was administered for Malaria in India, it may be the key to the cure." "A key to the cure, is that right, let me see what I can do to help you gain access." Mr. Lee said excitedly.

"Thank you, Mr. Lee, I'll let you go for now; however, I'll contact you in a few days, talk to you later, and thank you again." We disconnected after our conversation. I was going to tell Mr. Lee about the theory we had about mixing the drug Hydroxychloroquine and blood plasma from the recoveries of this virus. I believe this will work, but we just need blood from some survivors. I decided not to tell him for some reason unknown to me. Maybe I didn't want to get his and my hopes up to high without trying the two to see if it will work. Along with that, we still need to get the drug approved and able to use it on humans. Then a thought crossed my mind, I hope Mr. Lui Pand survives, and if he does, I can use the plasma from his blood or *Mi* Dem's.

I turned on the TV to see what was going on in the news. Deaths were reported everywhere and by great numbers. People were dying at alarming rates. I decided to call Shareen. "Hello Shareen, are you by chance watching the news?" "Hello Mr. Vector, unfortunately yes, what is going on, is Mr. Wu going around infected everyone he's in contact with?" She asked. "I'm not sure, but I know one thing; this virus is more contagious than anything I've ever seen or heard of,"

"Did you get a chance to talk to Mr. Lee?" "Yes, I did and he sounded concerned, he wants us to return home immediately," "NO, we can't do that yet, you did tell him, right?" "Yes, I explained to him we needed more time to develop a cure, he said he would only give us a few more weeks and that's all."

"We need more time than that, does he know how deadly this virus is, did you tell him about the possibility of Mr. Wu being out there somewhere infecting people on purpose and he may strike the United States of America, next?"

"Well actually I didn't go into detail with him, although I did fill him in with a lot of what's going on," "Why didn't you tell him everything Mr. Vector?" "I just didn't want to get my hopes up about anything." "Your hopes up, what are you talking about?" "Well I did ask him about the drug Hydroxychloroquine, and he said he would try to get access for us to use in our research,"

"That's great, but why didn't you fill him in with everything, wait, are you thinking Mr. Lee knew about all this mess?" "I'm not saying that, but I noticed how rude he was to me the last time we Skyped, and at this point, I don't trust anyone except you and my wife." "I appreciate that Mr. Vector, okay I'm on your side, and now what's next?"

"While Mr. Lui tries to get his hands on some Hydroxychloroquine, we have to make sure *Mi* Dem and Mr. Lui Pand recovers, so we can take their blood from them and use their antibodies to find a cure, maybe just maybe; if one or both make it, they will help save lives, but we need their blood plasma."

"Should we tell Sabian?" "I guess we can advise him of some discoveries, but not all, I still don't trust him." "I can understand that, he's still a kiss ass." Said Shareen.

"I do you agree, okay we can head to the hospital tomorrow and check to see how everything is doing; besides, I'm going to see if the doctors at the hospital have some Hydroxychloroquine in stock there." "Okay Mr. Vector, I'll talk with you tomorrow." Shareen said as she hung up the phone.

The next day we went back to the hospital. Mr. Lui Pand seemed to be stabilizing. *Mi* Dem was on the ventilator; however, the doctors felt she would come through because her vitals were improving.

I pulled the head Doctor over whom name was Mr. Bai Chang and I asked him did he have Hydroxychloroquine on hand in the hospital. He said he only had a little dose of it which he could get his hands on it. I explained to him I was a Scientist and I was already searching for a cure. He said he would get some for me. That's just what I needed, and now all I need is for Mr. Lui Pand to get well.

About a week later, Mr. Lui Pand started recovering and he was sitting up and talking. Everyone still had to wear protected gear while there. As I was telling Mr. Lui Pand how we were coming along, Mr. Bai Chang called me outside of the room. "I got a small dose of Hydroxychloroquine for you, here and don't let anyone know I got this for you." He whispered as he slowly placed a small vial in my hand.

"Thank you, Mr. Bai Chang, I'll keep it to myself," I grabbed the small vial and stuck it in my pocket. He walked away and I went back into the room to talk to Mr. Lui Pand, but he was fast asleep. Sabian and Shareen walked out of the room to stretch their legs some. I slowly walked over to Mr. Lui Pand and I pulled a small needle out of my pocket and I stuck it in the vial of Hydroxychloroquine. Then I injected a small dose in Mr. Lui Pand's vein in his arm. *I hope this helps him,* I said to myself.

Within a few days, Mr. Lui Pand recovered. They kept him in the hospital for a few more weeks under observation. Before I got the chance to try the Hydroxychloroquine on *Mi* Dem, she died.

Suddenly the hospitals were over flooded with people fighting for their lives from this virus. The number was soaring and we were in the middle of war, *a war with an airborne enemy!*

...For nearly two weeks the Chinese people were seeing their family members perish to an invisible enemy called Coronavirus. They then named it COVID 19...19 because it was the 19th strain of the flu, but it

was much more deadly. Me and my team fought diligently to find a cure. With the little dose of Hydroxychloroquine; we had we came up with a small dose of a cure. We tested it on some animals, yet we still came up with the same results, it worked on some of the animals; but some it didn't. The only positive result we had to fall back on was the fact it worked on Mr. Lui Pand. Maybe, just maybe, this cure can save some lives or contain the virus. Until now, it remained to be seen...

Chapter 6

Facing an airborne Enemy

{Six}

They let Mr. Lui Pand go home from the hospital. But he had to stay quarantined for a while; so of course, Mr. Tan Saki was still in charge. Truthfully, we didn't see much of him anyway. Just maybe, that was a good thing.

The news didn't have anything good to report. The virus was killing everyone in sight and the hospitals were becoming overwhelmed with sick patients. I called Sabian and Shareen for a meeting in the lobby of the hotel where I expressed my concerns and what we must do.

Mr. Lee had only promised us three weeks and we were now into our second week. We all sat down with frustrated looks on our faces and for a few seconds we were just speechless. By now, thousands had died and we still didn't have a vaccine. I realized at that time this might take us up to a year or more. My mind started wondering; I blew a big breath and spoke up.

"This is getting worse; I think we should find Mr. Wu and put an end to this madness." "Do you think he's out there still infecting people on purpose?" Shareen asked. "How do we find him and when we do, what should we do, attack him, hell no, I don't know about doing that, and take a risk of him affecting me with the virus." Said Sabian.

"I haven't thought about it, but we must detain him somehow, and call the authorities, let's go back to the market where he purchased the bats at, he might be there." I suggested. "Right, right," Shareen said.

"Maybe that Chinese boy name Wey, seen him or know where he's at, but like I said, if we see him, who's detaining that asshole, you Mr. Vector?" Sabian asked.

"We'll do something, hell I will put my life on the line for other people's lives," Shareen said. "And, so will I, Sabian what do you say, are you going with us?" "Yes, I'm going, but you guys can take him down yourselves, I'm not fucking with him." Sabian said. "Your kiss ass, chicken shit," said Shareen. "Whatever, let's go and find Mr. Wu, come on super woman." Sabian said with sarcasm.

"Guys please, no more name calling, we must find him, because if what he's doing ever make it to America, this won't be pretty, now let's get serious here." "And, we definitely don't want this virus to break out in America, whatever we have to do, we've got to stop him, and, now." Shareen said.

We headed out on our mission to find Mr. Wu. On our way there in one part of the city, we saw the bodies of homeless dead people laying on top of each other as trucks pulled up to put them in and take them way. It was a chilling sight. I'd never seen anything like this before. So many people were coughing even though they were wearing masks. All we could do is look at one another and shake our heads. We knew then we needed to stop Mr. Wu before he destroyed his own country.

In spite of people dying, the market was still filled with people. As we walked through the market, so many people looked ill. There's no way these people should've been out in these streets and besides, they may be infecting the food with all their coughing and sneezing.

From right to left these owners were trying to sell all the domestic animals they could. Sabian damn near threw up as he started gaging, by just looking at a man at storefront skinning huge rats and cutting the tails and head off in front of us.

“Sabian, are you okay?” I asked. He spit up and he bent down with both hands on his knees. “I’m okay, let’s hurry and find this guy and get the hell out of here, please,” yelled Sabian. “We’re almost there; I think I see the storefront where they sell the bats,” said Shareen.

“Good, I’m ready to go, hey don’t cough like that,” Sabian yelled as an old Chinese man didn’t cover his mouth. It’s a good thing we had our masks on. As we passed him, we turned around and the crowd made a loud cry. We turned around and the old Chinese man dropped dead right there in the market. We kept walking as some authorities with full protective gear picked up his limp body and took him away.

“This is crazy,” Sabian said. “We’re here I think, yeah this is it,” Shareen said. “Look around and see if you recognize anyone who even resembles Mr. Wu.” I said. “Mr. Vector, do you really think he’s that imprudent to come back here even if he knows the authorities are looking for him?” Shareen asked.

“This is definitely the place, look at those nasty ass bats, how in the hell do people eat this stuff?” Sabian asked with his nose turned up.

“Hey Sir, do you know Mr. Wu?” I asked a storefront owner. He didn’t appear to know how to speak any English, because he started speaking in his language and at the same time, he was still trying to sell us bats. “I don’t think he understands, no I don’t want any.” Shareen said as she hit the bat away from her face as the storefront owner was trying to sell it to her.

Then we noticed the little boy Wey standing with some little Chinese boys and Sabian called out to him. “Hey Wey, come here.” He commanded. Wey remembered who we were and gradually walked over and he had a mask on.

“Hey, it is the Americans, what is going on, you decided to buy the bats anyway?” Said Wey. “No way, we have a few questions to ask you.” Sabian said. “How much are you going to pay for the answers?” Wey asked. “Oh, we have to pay you?” Asked Shareen. “Hey lady there isn’t anything in this world for free.”

“Mr. Vector pay him what he wants.” Sabian said and I looked at him like he was crazy. “Why don’t you pay him, he’s your little friend.” I said with sarcasm. “Hey someone better pay me because I do not have all day, now which of you is it, come on now, we all know Americans got lots of money.” “I don’t know about all that.” Said Shareen.

“Okay look, I am going to pay you, but you better not lie or withhold any information about what you know, do you understand?” I asked. “Okay bet, what do you need to know?” Wey said as he put his hand out for some money. I put a few dollars in his hand first before I started asking him questions.

“Do you know a man named Mr. Wu?” “Of course, I know Mr. Wu, everyone knows him around here, and he works with Mr. Lui Pand at Pandemica Compound.” Wey said. “Have you seen him around here?” Shareen asked and Wey held his hand out again for more money.

“You are definitely a business man, I like that.” said Sabian with a smirk on his face. I pulled out more money and stared Sabian down. “You would like that Sabian, because it’s not your money you’re giving up, now Wey, have you seen Mr. Wu around the market lately?” I asked as I put more money in his hand.

“Cheap ass.” Sabian whispered and I just gave him a fuck you look. “Sabian, knock it off, this is serious business,” Said Shareen.

“To answer your question, no I have not seen him around, the word around here is, the authorizes are looking for him, and it was said he was going out of the country too perhaps to Italy, or France, or something like that.” Said Wey. I grabbed him by his shirt and choked him up. “Where did you hear this from?” I demanded as I looked dead into his eyes, to cause a little fear.

“Hey, hey, let me go, I am only telling you what I know, I just know they said he was implying he was going to change the world; you know talking really senseless like he lost his mind or something.”

"So, you heard all of that, but you haven't seen him, huh, Wey is that what you want us to believe?" Sabian said and Wey just put out his hands for money again. "You, you little fucker, you." Sabian snickered.

"Damn this kid, here, take the money and this is all you're getting." I said furiously. "Hey, take it easy American, I am trying to tell you something here, relax, I am not lying about a thing, and since you are so generous, I will tell you this for free, do you know Mr. Tan Saki, Mr. Wu's friend, well he was here in the market buying domestic animals including the bats." Wey said with a serious expression. "Generous my eye." Shareen said as she stood there with her arms crossed.

"Hold up, why would Mr. Tan Saki buy fucking bats?" Sabian asked. "I do not know genius, maybe he eats them, like I said he bought other domestic animals also." Wey said while being cynical.

"Oh my God, do you guys think Mr. Tan Saki is in on this?" I asked. "I don't know, Mr. Vector, what do you think?" Shareen asked. "Can you let me go now, besides that little bit of money you just gave me, lets me know you are a cheap shit." Wey said as I released his shirt. He started walking away while counting the money I gave him.

"Hey kid," Shareen said. "What, that is all I know." Wey said while gradually walking backwards. "Where did you learn how to speak English so well?" Shareen asked. "I learned at school, duh."

Wey said as he ran away laughing. "Oh, smart ass," Shareen said. "Well, you asked." Sabian said while laughing deafeningly.

"This is serious, we can't let Mr. Wu continue to spread this virus." Shareen said. Suddenly, my mind started wondering. "You're right and I just thought of something." "Can we get the hell out of here?" Sabian asked. "Yes, let's get back to the lab, there's something I need to research," I said.

"Okay, about time, let's get out of here." Shareen said. "And, away from this revolting looking food, ewe," Sabian said. We left the market and we went back to the hotel. I called to check on Mr. Lui Pand. He was recovering well. I ask him would we be able to work at the lab in the morning and he said he would tell Mr. Tan Saki to let us in Pandemica so we can continue our research. Although I wasn't too sure about Mr. Tan Saki, I knew I had to find out some more information and do thorough research. I didn't want to say anything about what I knew to Mr. Lui Pand, so I just left it at that.

Early the next morning the cars were there to pick us up and when we got to Pandemica, Mr. Tan Saki was there to let us in. Neither one of us said anything to him. We went straight to the lab. I told Shareen and Sabian what my thoughts were, but first we had to dissect one of the rats which died from the virus. I needed to learn more about this virus.

Then, we did just that, and what I found amazed me. The virus is attacking the lungs of its host in this case the rat. It's filling the lungs up with fluid which makes it difficult to breath and the rat then dies; as it kills off the major cells in the lungs which allows them to breath oxygen in and carbon monoxide out.

"This is all good information, Mr. Vector," Shareen said. "Are we still going to look for Mr. Wu?" Sabian asked. "No, we don't have time, we'll let the authorities catch him, I think right now this virus is mutating and traveling on its own from people to people, rather from hand-to-hand contact or air particles, you know as if someone coughs or sneezes."

"So, what do we do now?" Shareen asked. "Let's get out of here, I have to talk to Mr. Lee, we may just be out of time," I said as we gathered up all our work and headed out. Mr. Tan Saki came from out of nowhere and asked, "Are you leaving already?" "Yes, can you please escort us out?" I asked. He shook his head up and down and then walked us out. As we were getting in our cars, we heard Mr. Tan Saki began to bend over and start to cough. We hurried and got in our cars. I turned back and he was still coughing and we pulled off, I could see him stand straight up and instantly stop coughing as he had this evil look on his face. I was mystified.

I thought about it all the way to the hotel. *It was unquestionably something to take a mental note on.*

Chapter 7

Made it out before Lockdown

{Seven}

When we made it back to the hotel, we sat in the lobby to discuss a few things, I wasn't sure if Shareen and Sabian had seen Mr. Tan Saki and the crazy stunt he had just pulled. I asked them and they both said they saw the same thing. At that point, we were all bewildered as to what was going on.

"Listen, I think Mr. Tan Saki has something to do with all this, but I can't put my finger on it?" I said. "I believe also, maybe he and Mr. Wu are in this together." Shareen said. "I don't know, I never ever seen them together, other than when we were all together at the lab." Sabian said.

"Well, I know you just seen him coughing and then suddenly stop as we pulled off, now what was that all about?" I asked. "Do you think he was faking in order to throw us off?" Sabian asked. "It could be a plot, what do you think Mr. Vector?" Shareen asked. "I really don't know, that remains to be seen, but we have a bigger problem on our hands, because after I talk to Mr. Lee, we may have to get back to the United States." I said.

"And, leave that fucking mad man Mr. Wu out here spreading this virus?" Sabian asked. "Unfortunately, yes, there may be another way to stop him, but as for now we must stop this Pandemic from reaching America." I said. "I agree, but how will we do that?" Shareen asked.

"That's a good question," Sabian said. "Yes, a good question, but first I need to tell you guys what happened at the hospital," I said. "What, happened, did you hear or see anything?" Sabian asked. "What, tell us Mr. Vector?" Shareen asked with curiosity. I folded my arms and walked around for a second before I spoke.

"Remember when you guys walked out to stretch your legs, when Mr. Lui Pand was in bad shape in the hospital?" "Yes, I believe so,"

Sabian said. “Well?” Shareen questioned. “While you all were out, I injected Mr. Lui Pand with our sample vaccine and it made him recover from the virus, at least I think it did help.” “You did what, it could have backfired on you and could have killed him, we haven’t had proper testing yet.” Sabian said loudly as he brushed his hand through his head and started pacing.

“You’re right, but it didn’t backfire, it worked, right Mr. Vector, it worked.” Said Shareen. “He is alive and recovering, so I guess it didn’t do any harm,” I said. “Listen Mr. Vector, you can’t take something this large and important into your own hands without proper testing and experimenting with these drugs.” Sabian loudly said. “What the fuck, what the fuck, fuck, fuck.” Sabian repeated with a pause in between words.

“Sabian, knock it off, the drug didn’t cause any harm, we can’t just stand around and watch people die.” I said. “Mr. Vector I’m glad you made that bold choice, but we have to be very careful with this drug.” Shareen said. “Especially for the people who have a pre-existing condition such as, a heart problem, weakened immune system issues, or even diabetes,” Sabian said.

“How do you know all this?” I asked. “While you two were working together, I was working on my own research and found some rats were stronger and they survived, but the ones that were already filled with sickness died and I mean some of them died fucking instantly." "Well thanks for telling us now," I said with sarcasm. "I told you, didn't I?" Sabian said with derision.

"Guys enough, we can't solve anything with division amongst us, all we can do is learn from this and move on, now shall we?" Shareen said. After that heated discussion, we decided to call it the night and go to our rooms. I immediately got on my computer and did some more research on the drugs we could possibly try and also gathered data from past Pandemics, like the Pandemic of 1918. Millions died back then. Sometimes, history repeats itself, so it's always good to go back and find data that could help in the future and that was my goal.

I stayed up until the wee hours of the morning doing research. Finally, morning came and I was falling asleep on my laptop; only to jump right back up and proceed to keep working. I turned on the news and made some coffee. The onslaught of deaths was spiking. I put my head in my hands and tears rolled out of my eyes. This is even worse than any one of us could have ever imagined.

A news alert appeared on the screen and it reported Mr. Wu was wanted and being sought by the authorities and he needed to be brought in for questioning. They labeled him dangerous, so proceed to take him with caution. He was last seen in Italy. When I heard that news it gave me chills. He is planning to infect the world with some kind of chemical warfare. *This isn't good!* I thought to myself.

The news hit me like a ton of bricks. How could someone be so heartless and not care about anyone else's lives? The news continued; after watching a commercial, the Reporter said Wuhan Officials were considering doing a total lockdown and, in a few days, they would stop all international travel. We must leave before then or we may never make it back to the United States. Time was now running out. I knew at that point I needed to call Mr. Lee.

I proceeded to log onto Skype to speak with Mr. Lee. He finally answered the video call. For some reason he was ranting about the authorities wanting to bring him in about withholding vital information from United States Officials. I really couldn't understand everything he was saying. After his rant, I told him that he needed to send our plane tickets so we could leave China.

"Mr. Lee, it's time for us to pack it up here, we did all we could do." "I will purchase your plane tickets right after we are done talking, so there isn't anything else you guys can do there?" "No, we did all we could do, except…" "Except what Mr. Vector?" "We wanted to catch up to Mr. Wu and have him detained by the authorities; apparently he is the key to all this psychosis going on, and word is, he's traveling to different countries to continue spreading the virus."

"That damn idiot." "Yes, he is a damn idiot and more, but also don't forget he's a dangerous man and he must be stopped." "I will have you guys out of there by tomorrow afternoon, now get all your belongings ready, you can finish researching for a cure here."

"Wow, that fast, I need to tell Shareen and Sabian as soon as I get off here with you." "There is one thing I need you to do." "What's that Mr. Lee?" "There is Surgeon by the name of Mathew Lee Su there at the hospital, he has some top-secret files for me, please go pick them up as soon as possible, I will let him know you are coming."

"What's so top-secret about these files?" "Never mind that, just please pick them up for me." *What's so top-secret about these files?* I wondered. Once again Mr. Lee went on another rant about people wanting to question him about some underhanded procedures they suspect he's doing.

"Mr. Lee, are you doing these things you've been accused of?" "No, I am not guilty of any wrong doing, hey but that is another story for another day, make sure you go see Mathew Lee Su and get the files." "I'll make sure to pick them up, is there anything else?"

"Yes, I have a question, have anyone of you had spoken to Mr. Tan Saki as of lately?" "No, we haven't, why Mr., Lee?" "He is my nephew and he has been missing for days now." Hearing Mr. Tan Saki was Mr. Lee's family member floored me. *What the hell is going on here?* I thought to myself.

"The last time I saw him he was at the lab and when we were leaving Sir, he was coughing, I believe." "He was coughing you believe? What does that mean Mr. Vector?" "Well, nothing Sir, well I'll let everyone know we'll be leaving tomorrow, I'll get packed and will talk to you later." "Mr. Vector, Mr. Vector…" Mr. Lee called out to me, but I pretended as if we lost connection and disconnected our Skype conversation on purpose. I immediately called Shareen and told her to start packing and be ready to leave the next day and to contact Sabian advising him of the same instructions.

I received a phone call from an unfamiliar voice. "Hello, who is this?" I asked. "This is Mathew Lee Su, your Boss Mr. Lee gave me your number and asked me to call you, I have some important files he wants me to give you, is an hour good for you to come pick them up?" He asked. "Oh, yes, I'm on my way."

"Thank you, kindly meet me in the rear parking lot, I will be in a dark blue Mercedes parked near the back-entrance door, see you soon." I headed to the hospital to pick up the top-secret files from Mathew Lee Su. As the driver pulled in the rear-parking lot, I saw Mathew Lee Su's Mercedes. I parked next to him. I jumped out the car and jumped into his car. He was wearing bifocals; nerdy-looking glasses and a very thick mask on his face.

"Mr. Vector I presume?" "Yes, Mathew, I presume?" "Here are the files Mr. Lee asked for." "Do you know what's inside them?" "If I did, then they would not be top-secret files Mr. Vector." "Can you tell me anything, after all I am putting my life in jeopardy by even coming here." I said. As we were conversing, a forklift rode by with a coffin box and a dead body in it and loaded it on a refrigerated truck. Then another forklift rode by with another coffin box.

"Man, I can't take this, so many people are dying, well just know this, these files may save lives so there is not anything in them which may put your life or your love ones in any kind of danger." Mathew said with a sound of anguish. "I know this is getting overwhelming for you here at the hospital," I said. "Yes, it is and each day it is getting worse, so far today 575 people just died and the day is not near being over, oh my God, my poor people."

"I feel so sorry and helpless, I don't know if Mr. Lee told you me and my team are conducting research for a cure." "He did tell me, you were one of his finest Scientists, and I hope you do find this cure Mr. Vector, before this plague wipe all humanity out."

"Well, I must be going, I have a plane to catch tomorrow." "Leaving so soon?" "Yes, Mr. Lee got our tickets already, but I'll be back with a cure, I can promise you that." "I believe you Mr. Vector, here, is my number, we can keep in touch and one other thing."

"What's that?" "Can you tell Mr. Lee; Mr. Tan Saki came to give me a visit a few days ago, I know he is Mr. Lee's nephew." "Mr. Tan Saki came to see you, how was he feeling, was he sick?" "Actually no, but he was acting strange and for some reason he was trying to get me to give him these files." "But, why?" "I cannot tell you why, but I was not about to do that, I told him he should leave and he did."

"I know he's Mr. Lee's nephew, but I don't trust him, I've never trusted him, there's something about him that's just not right, he left without saying anything else to you?" "I told him I had to get back to work and he had to leave and then I left my office."

"Then what happened?" "I left and so did he, but when I returned back to my office it was ram shacked, I am not sure if it was his doing, but he was the last one I spoke with." "Do you think he was trying to steal the top-secret files?" "Perhaps, but I had taken them with me and locked them in a secured place, in my safe."

"I'm not so sure if I should tell Mr. Lee this news, but listen, I'll be in touch with you, it's time for me to get things together, I wish you all the best here." I said as I got out of his car and started talking to him through the car window. As we said goodbye to one another, I couldn't help thinking about what were in these files and why was Mr. Tan Saki was trying to steal them.

When I got back to the hotel, I filled the guys in about our flight, but I didn't tell them about the top-secret files. The next day we were on a plane heading back to the United States. We made it out just in time, because at midnight China went on a nationwide lockdown for thirty days. No one was getting in and no one was going out!

Chapter 8

The Virus spreads to America

{Eight}

Our plane finally landed back to America. I immediately called Mr. Lee as we walked out of the airport and got into a taxi, but I received no answer. I called him over and over again. "You still can't get a hold of Mr. Lee?" Shareen asked. "That's not like Mr. Lee not to answer his damn phone." Said Sabian.

"I don't know what's going on, but I'll try again later, I miss my wife and children." I said. The taxi dropped each one of us home and I was so glad to be home especially after seeing all the deaths in China. Chancie, the children and my dog Scruffy met me at the door and they gave me a great big hug. I was so pleased to see them. It's been a while. Home never felt so good. Later on, that night, I told Chancie everything that was going on and she insisted I tell someone in authority, even if it was the President of the United States. *How am I supposed to get what I know to the President, and, will he listen to me?* That was my thought. At the same time our President Daniel T. Crump was going through an impeachment. It was said he had some shady dealings with the Ukrainians and the Russians. It was an ongoing investigation. *With all that on his plate, would he even listen to what I have to say?*

My mind was filled with these thoughts and I barely even slept that night. Early the next morning, I tried to call Mr. Lee again, but once again, I got no answer. I decided to go to my job at Stanley F. Pharmaceuticals, to see if he was there.

I stopped at the front desk and I talked to our Receptionist. Her name was Mrs. Ingram. She was a very nice lady and usually kind, but this morning she was moody and distraught.

"Mrs. Ingram have you seen or talked to Mr. Lee?" "Oh my God, haven't you heard Mr. Vector?" "Heard, heard what?" "The Feds came in and they took Mr. Lee to jail, they say he's funding Terrorists or have something to do with a conspiracy against the United States of America, he's being held by the Feds." She said as she whimpered with tears rolling down her face.

"Say what, no, I just got back in the country last night, as a matter-of-fact Mr. Lee got our plane tickets for us to get back here." "You mean the tickets for you, Mr. Vector, Sabian and Shareen?" "Yes, I just talked to him a couple of days ago, I think it was, yes, just a day or so ago." "Well, I'm the one who made the arrangements for the plane tickets, Mr. Lee asked me to do that right before the Feds came and took him out, I don't know what to do, this has to be a mistake, Mr. Lee has been nothing but good to me."

"Yes, this has to be some kind if mix-up, I'll have to get back with you later, if you hear anymore news, please contact me, here." I said as I passed Mrs. Ingram my business card.

Then as I was walking towards the door, a loud noise rang out and glass flew everywhere. I instantly hit the floor as I heard loud voices saying, "You traitor, you fucking traitors." The voices came from a big red tow truck as it struck the front lobby of Stanley F. Pharmaceuticals. They quickly sped off.

“Mrs. Ingram call the police, please call them now,” I yelled. Mrs. Ingram slowly stood up from behind the desk and hurried to call 911. The police came fast and we explained what happened and I told them about the red truck. They went looking for whoever did this and I left the building for fear they would come back.

I called Shareen and told her about the incident and what happened to Mr. Lee. She was just about as bewildered as I was. What, no, Mr. Lee couldn’t have turned on our country, we must go see where he’s at and talk to him; I’ll find out more about this and will get back with you Mr. Vector.” “Okay, I’ll talk to you later, let me call Sabian to inform him about what’s going on.” “Good luck, because I haven’t been able to contact him all day long, it’s like he went missing also.”

“Really, well let me see if I can get through to him, talk to you later,” I said as I hung up the line with her. I instantly called Sabian’s phone. His phone rang and rang, but no answer. I headed back home.

When I pulled up to the driveway, I noticed an unknown car parked in front of my house. I put the key into the door and opened it. As I walked in, there was Sabian and a Chinese man. He was the same man I saw him passing papers too in the lobby of the hotel were we staying at in China. They were sitting on the sofa and Chancie was handing them some water to drink.

"Chancie, honey, can you please excuse us and keep the children in their bedrooms." I said with carefulness. Chancie headed upstairs and I slowly sat down on the sofa. I was caught off guard and I really didn't know what this was about and I had to make sure I safely secured my family.

"Mr. Vector, look, please don't be alarmed," Said Sabian. "I am beyond alarmed, that you would show up at my home unannounced, what's going on and who is this?" I asked. "Mr. Vector, I am Detective Hue Sun." The Chinese man said in proper English.

"So, you're American?" I asked. "Yes, Chinese American and I work for the American government." He said with a grim voice. "Mr. Vector, Detective Hue Sun has been on this case for a while now, and I have just been assisting him, by giving him all the information I found out while in China." Sabian said.

"Information, information for what, and what case?" I asked. "Mr. Vector, there was some information indicating Mr. Lee was sending American intelligence information to China, so China can one day become the richest country in the world, we had to make sure that wasn't the case."

"So, this is about Mr. Lee, well do you know he's been arrested?" I asked. "He hasn't been arrested yet, but he is being questioned." Sabian said. "That's what Mrs. Ingram told me." I said. "She's just hysterical, she doesn't know any better, she's just shook up." said Sabian.

"Mr. Vector, we are here because we believe we have enough evidence to get Mr. Lee freed from the authorities." Mr. Hue Sun said. "Okay, well let's find out where Mr. Lee is and take them all the information you guys found." I suggested.

"Alright, but first we need to know is there any information you found that may help him any further?" Asked Sabian. I got up and paced the floor with my hand on my chin. I was contemplating on should I tell them everything I knew. But my conscience kept telling me, to don't say a thing, so I didn't. "No, I don't know much, so shall we go and get Mr. Lee out of this jam?" I asked. Sabian and Mr. Hue Sun looked at each other and they both stood up.

"Yes, let's go see what we can do." Sabian said. "Alright, we should have enough information and evidence to get M. Lee out of this situation." Said Mr. Hue Sun.

I jumped in my car and I followed Sabian and Detective Hue Sun. We ended up in a secluded Federal compound where the Feds interrogate prisoners. Sabian and Detective Hue Sun were able to get us to see Mr. Lee. He was happy to see us as they sat us in a dark room with guards posted everywhere. His face was bruised and he looked like he had been beaten. I turned and looked at the guards and asked, "Who did this to him?" They didn't say a word.

“Mr. Vector, never mind, I am okay, Mr. Hue Sun, it’s good to see you, and Sabian, I hope you guys are going to get me out of here.” Mr. Lee said with nervousness in his voice. “That’s why we’re here Mr. Lee.” Sabian said. “We are here to get you out, Sir.” Detective Hue Sun said as he started breathing intensely.

“Mr. Lee, may I ask why are they accusing you of espionage?” I asked. “Mr. Vector, I believe because they found out Tan Saki is my nephew and he is now wanted by authorities.” “But that doesn’t mean you had anything to do with this crazy shit.” Said Sabian. “That’s what I was trying to tell them, but they did not believe me because the Feds said they saw Mr. Wu leaving my office a few days ago.” Mr. Lee said while looking clueless.

“Hold up, wait a minute Mr. Wu is in America?” Detective Hue Sun asked. “That is what the Feds said, but I swear I never saw him and I do not know why he would come all the way from China just to come see me in America.” Mr. Lee said.

“Are you sure Mr. Lee, I mean why would he come to see you?” I asked. “Yes, I am sure, maybe he was looking for…for, oh hell, I do not know, anyway can you guys get me out of here?”

After our conversation, Sabian and Directive Hue Sun went to provide the proof they had that Mr. Lee was innocent. Mr. Lee looked at me, whispered, and said, “I believe Mr. Wu was looking for the secret files, that I had you retain from Mathew Lee Su.”

"Oh my God, if what you say is true, then we are already in trouble, because Mr. Wu is here and he's out there somewhere spreading the virus, we must stop him." I said in a whisper. "Do you have the secret files Mr. Vector?" "Yes, I have them in a safe place, damn, I wonder what's taking Sabian and Detective Hue Sun so long?" I said.

Suddenly the door flew open, and Mr. Lee was free to go. I don't know what information they provided to free Mr. Lee, but it must have been legit. Mr. Lee rode with me and Sabian and Detective Hue Sun drove in the other direction. As soon as I turned a few corners, we spotted Mr. Wu in a Mercedes driving to opposite way. "There is Mr. Wu, turn around, turn around," Mr. Lee yelled. "I see him, I see him," I said as I made a quick U-turn. Mr. Wu's eyes locked to mine and he started flooring his car. He was going so fast; it was hard for me to keep up with him.

"You're letting him get away," Mr. Lee yelled. "I'm trying to catch him, I'm trying." I was about five car lengths behind and Mr. Wu ran a red light, another car came out of nowhere, hit the back of his car, his car began spinning around in circles and finally he hit a store front near an alleyway. Mr. Wu jumped out and ran. Mr. Lee and I jumped out and we gave chase.

Mr. Wu ran down an alley where several homeless people were laying on mattresses. He stuck a needle in two of the homeless guys as he ran by them. Mr. Lee and I tried to stop him. Then he grabbed a homeless lady and he put a needle to her neck as he held her in a choke hold.

“You son of a bitch, you stuck me with that needle.” The homeless man said as he immediately started coughing out of control. “Muthafuckers, why you stick me?” The second homeless man yelled as he grabbed his neck. “Mr. Wu let her go, please, just turn yourself in, it’s over,” I said. “You don’t get to tell me when it’s fucking over, dammit, it is over when I say it is over, Mr. Vector do you hear me, now move out my damn way before I inject her with the virus.” Shouted Mr. Wu.

“Mr. Wu, Let her go and stop this madness, now dammit.” Mr. Lee said as he tried to sound convincing. Mr. Wu started walking towards us with the homeless lady in his grasp. “Where are the secret files, I need them and I need them now,” Mr. Wu yelled out. “No, you’re not getting anything,” I said. “How do you know about the files?” Mr. Lee asked. “Never mind that give them to me, if you do not, I will inject her now.”

“Please don’t’ hurt me,” the homeless lady was able to squeak out of her mouth as his grasp around her neck kept her from screaming and yelling. The other two homeless men jumped up and started running out of the alley as they both started coughing profusely. “Stop,

stop." I yelled out to stop the homeless men because I knew they could possibly pass the virus around. They kept running.

"Mr. Lee, I will get those secret files," Mr. Wu said. Suddenly we heard police sirens. Mr. Wu's eyes got wide and big. He ran through us after he injected the homeless lady in the arm with the needle and threw her at the both of us. We couldn't catch Mr. Wu. The sirens were getting closer, Mr. Lee and I hurried towards the car.

"What should we do with her." Mr. Lee asked. "We have to leave her; she has been infected and she might pass it on to us." I said. The homeless lady laid on the ground and she began coughing and crying. I felt so bad for her, but there wasn't anything we could do for her and we got out of there before the police arrived.

About five police cars passed us as we left the scene. Mr. Lee and I looked straight ahead so we wouldn't bring any attention to ourselves. "Mr. Lee, may I ask you a question?" "What is on your mind Mr. Vector, damn, I hate that we let Mr. Wu get away." Said Mr. Lee. "I hate it also, but can you tell me, how in the hell did Mr. Wu know about the secret files?" "I do not know, perhaps my nephew Tan Saki, told him about the files." He implied.

"What's in the file's Sir, and why would they be so important to Mr. Wu?" I asked. But Mr. Lee didn't answer, instead he just shrugged his shoulders up and down. "When will you bring the secret files to me?" Asked Mr. Lee. I did the exact same thing he did to me, I sat quietly and I just shrugged my shoulders. I can tell it infuriated Mr. Lee. But I didn't care. I felt there was something fishy going in with this whole situation.

I had the files in a safe place and there wasn't a thing that anybody could do about it. Besides, I figured Mr. Wu wouldn't expect me to have them. I dropped Mr. Lee off at his house. He got out of my car and turned and he asked, "When will you give me the secret files, Mr. Vector?" "Soon, I have them in a safe place, don't worry."

I pulled off and I headed home and it started to rain very hard. I sped up my windshields so I could see ahead of me. The rain got harder as I made my way home. I hurried up and ran inside of the house, then I headed right to my safe. I pulled the files out and stared at them.

I decided at that point I must see what's inside. As I was about to open them my phone rang. I placed the files back in my safe and I answered the phone. It was Shareen, she was crying, and she was hysterical. Shareen said she was heading to the hospital because Mr. Wu had broken into her house with her in it looking for the secret files. He injected her with the virus. I could barely understand her as she cried and coughed at the same time. I tried to calm her down, but she wouldn't listen to me so I told her to make sure she lets me know when she gets to the hospital and to keep me posted. I couldn't believe it. As I sat down on the sofa, I turned on the TV. I was in disbelief. The news showed a clip of lots of sick people entering the hospital and they couldn't figure out why so many people fell ill all at the same time. That moment I realized that the virus had now spread to America and we were in big trouble.

Chapter 9

We weren't Ready

{Nine}

Again, I took the files out of my safe. When I was about to open it, my phone rang once again, so I answered it. "Hello, who is this?" I said as I put the files back into my safe. "Mr. Vector, hello, this is Mathew Lee Su, I am calling you because I have contracted the virus and I am in the hospital." "Say what, how, what happened?"

“This virus is much more contagious than we thought, but do not worry about me I am okay, I will beat this virus.” Mathew Lee Su said he started coughing. “Mathew Lee Su, I have to tell you, Mr. Wu is in America and he is spreading the virus.”

“You must stop him, you must get this information to your President so he knows what is going on, because I am afraid your country will be overwhelmed if they are not prepared.” “Mathew Lee Su, can I ask you, what’s in the secret files?”

“When the time comes, you will know, I must go now, I am going to blow the whistle on Mr. Tan Saki and everything that occurred at the Pandemica Compound, Mr. Vector, I will keep in touch.” Mathew Lee Su said as he hangs up the phone while still coughing.

After hanging up I walked over to my safe and pushed the files back in there and walked upstairs to the bedroom. I showered and got in bed. “Honey, are you okay, what’s going on?” Chancie asked and then she kissed me in my cheek.

“Chancie, I don’t know what’s going on, everything is crazy, but there is something big coming our way.” “What do you mean, the way you’re talking is scaring me.” I filled her in with everything that was going on and she was frightened. I had to calm her down and I promised her everything would be alright.

I kissed her and she kissed me back. At that moment we both blocked out everything that was happening and we began making love.

I really needed it with all that was going on. It took my mind off everything for just one night. *I was on top of her and then I flipped her on top of me. She rode me and rode me. I grabbed her waist and then grabbed her perky breast; we both were breathing hard. Then as she rode me so strong, I started feeling my release and we both let go at the same time. It felt so good as we took the stress out and then we both fell asleep until morning.*

When we woke up, Chancie smiled and she said, “Honey, you need to let the President know what’s going on.” “I know, I’ll have Mrs. Ingram make our flight arrangements to go to D.C. tomorrow morning.” “Our, who else is going?” “I was thinking about asked Sabian.” “Honey, promise me something.” “What’s that Chancie?” “Please be safe honey, I don’t want anything to happen to you.” “I promise, I will be alright and I’ll be back to you.” I said as I kissed her gently.

Chancie got up to take a shower and I got up and went downstairs to make some coffee. After I made my coffee, I sat down and turned on the news. There was a live showing of the President going through an impeachment hearing with Congress. They were trying to get him out of the White House. *How am I going to get him to listen to me?* I thought to myself. I really didn’t know how, but I knew I had to because America needed to be prepared. Shortly after watching some of the trial, the Presidents’ Advisor was convicted for a crime and another named Bobby Shueller was sentenced in a Russian probe. It seemed as if they were all going down. That made my decision to tell the President even more difficult.

Then a breaking news alert came up on the scene. The reporter was in front of a hospital and she was talking about so many people getting sick. Then she said someone died because of this sickness. The reporter said a respiratory virus may be the cause. Then she said the first death came from a woman and then she said her name. She said the woman who died from the virus was Shareen Duvaye. I yelped and tears came down my eyes. I couldn't watch anymore.

Then my phone rang and it was Sabian. He said he just saw the news. My heart was hurt and we hung up the phone. Shortly after, Mr. Lee called me and he saw the news as well. I got off the phone with him and went upstairs and I started tearing until Chancie came over and held me, as I told her what happened to Shareen. I knew I had to let the President know what was going on.

The next morning, I called Sabian and I asked him to go with me to talk to the President of the United States. I asked him because he knew a lot of people in high places. I figured it was a good idea if I bought him a long; but I still didn't trust him. When we landed in D.C. my phone rang and it was Mathew Lee Su.

"Mr. Vector, did you tell your President yet?" "Hello Mathew Lee Su, my plane just landed and I plan on talking with the President today, how are you doing?" "I am still sick, but I am not in a good place right now." "Why, what do you mean, what's wrong?"

"I told the authorities what was going on at the Pandemica Compound and they said I was lying and I was just trying to get everyone in China in an uproar." "Say what, don't they know that you are trying to help them and save lives?" "I do not think they care, as a matter of fact they have officers at my room, outside the door and they are waiting until I feel better and they said they were going to arrest me."

"What the hell, I am sorry I can't help you, but I'll let the President know about you and tell him what is going on in your country." "Thank you, Mr. Vector, there is one more thing you should know, this virus is called COVID, from what I know it attacks the lungs and it causes an upper respiratory tract illness, it kills those with pre-existing illnesses and some people actually survive."

"How do you know all of this?" "I was also searching for a cure, that is something Mr. Lee and I both know, I decided to name the virus, CO for corona, VI for virus, D for disease and I refer it to the Novel Coronavirus." "Wow, I wonder why Mr. Lee didn't tell us what your connection was to this." "We kept it hidden and for good reason, I have to go now, you go ahead and try to save your country." We both then, hung up the phone.

“Mr. Vector, who the hell was that?” Sabian asked as we headed for our luggage. “Oh nothing, no one, no one,” I said. Sabian looked away and didn’t ask anything else until we went and got a rental car. He got on his phone as we headed to downtown D.C. Sabian was trying to get in touch with all his connections.

Finally, he got in touch with one of the President’s Advisors and he let him know the seriousness of what we knew. The President was holding a press conferences later that evening so we planned on telling him then. But first, we set out to get a hotel to get a little rest.

“My connection Mr. Vector, my connection said he would be able to arrange for us a direct conversation with the President after the press conference tonight, but until then, what hotel would you like to stay in?”

“Sabian, let’s try the Holiday Inn, but first let’s find some food, I am starved.” “I am too, what do you have taste for?” “I don’t know, let’s drive by some restaurants near the inner city.” We drove by a few restaurants until we came up to small Chinese restaurant. Sabian and I looked at each other and we both said, “No, no way.” We drove a little bit more until we saw a restaurant that served large plates of food, we decided to eat there. Theses plates were filled with a variety of meats and vegetables.

As we got out of the car, I noticed a black car pulled about three cars behind us. It pulled in the parking spot very slow. I didn’t know what to think of it, so went we stepped out of the car, I tried to be nosy. It seemed to be about four or five men in a black Charger and they looked of Asian descent, but I couldn't really get a good look because the windows were tinted. They appeared to be discussing something amongst each other. They didn't give us any eye contact as we got out and walked into the restaurant. I guess it was only coincidental, but I could've sworn they followed us there. *I just had a feeling!*

We sat down and ordered our large plates. Sabian and I conversed about what would we say to the President and we discussed the death of Shareen. It saddened me that Shareen was not here, but we both vowed to find this cure in her name. Our food finally came and I couldn't wait to sink my teeth into my large plate. Just as I took a bite, a man of Asian descent, dressed in all black clothes and dark black shades walked into the restaurant. My mouth froze when I was just about to bite into my food.

"What's wrong Mr. Vector, you look like you just saw a damn ghost?" Sabian said as he bit into his food. Then I finally bit into my food. "Nothing Sabian, I just had a thought." "A thought about what?" "It's nothing, I'll tell you later."

Sabian continued to eat his food as I watched the Asian man order five large plates of food. I was trying to see if he was watching us, but he kept looking straight ahead and also taking a glimpse of the menu he had in his hands.

"Mr. Vector, you seem jittery, are you sure everything is alright?" asked Sabian. I turned to see if anybody was listening, then I caught the Asian man peeking at us while holding his shades down and when he noticed me looking, he instantly let his shades drop down as if he wasn't paying any attention to us. I knew then I had to warn Sabian.

I whispered, "Sabian, see the Asian guy down there waiting on his food?" "Yeah, I see him, why Mr. Vector?" "I believe him and four other Asian men are following us and watching us." Sabian slowly turned his head to take a look at the Asian guy, but again he acted as if he wasn't paying us any attention.

"Mr. Vector are you fucking sure?" "Yes, I'm sure, I noticed them pulling up behind us when we parked to come in here." "Okay, we have to be very careful getting out of here, I wonder if they have a back door here, I'll ask the waiter when he comes by." quietly said Sabian.

"Are you sure, a back door, I don't know about going through the back door, what if the others are set up at the back door and they try to kill us or something?" "Calm down Mr. Vector and look under the table." "A gun, Sabian, you have a gun, where did you get that thing from?" "Relax, I have connections and I'm licensed to carry."

"Relax, how in the hell am I supposed to relax when there are men following us for God knows what and you have a gun?" I whispered in all nervousness. Sabian didn't even wait for the waiter to come by, he just got up and walked toward the waiter and pulled him to the side and they started talking. I could see the Asian guy staring at them while they were conversing. Sabian walked back over and said there weren't any back exits. *What were we going to do? I thought to myself.*

"What do you want to do, just walk out?" I asked. "We don't have any other choice." "Okay, I'm ready when you're ready."

"Let's go, now," Sabian said with force and we headed towards the door. The waiter was just about to hand the Asian guy his food and he turned to look at what we were doing and all of his food hit the floor. He didn't even pick his food up. He just marched swiftly behind Sabian and me.

"Hey, hey, do you see that car, head there and don't look back because I do have a gun." The Asian guy yelled with a Chinese accent. Then I could see Sabian clinch his gun on his hip, but I moved his hand and whispered. "Not yet." He looked at me as if I was crazy. I was just hoping I was going to find out what this was all about. We walked over to the car with the other Asian men in it and they were looking evil.

"Look, look, look in here, isn't this your friend?" The Asian guy said. Sabian and I both looked in the car as the window slowly rolled down. "Detective Hue Sun, oh my God are you alright?" I asked. These four men had Detective Hue Sun hands tied up, grey tape around his mouth, he was bleeding from the side of his eye and his mouth.

"Detective Hue Sun, what's going on, why are you doing this and who the hell are you?" Sabian yelled. "I will ask the damn questions; do you hear me?" The Asian guy said. "He is alright, we just beat his snooping ass a little and if you two don't give us what we fucking want, something bad is going to happen to your ass also." The Asian guy in the back seat of the car said as he sat very close to Detective Hue Sun.

"What are you talking about, give you what, we don't have anything." I said. "What the hell, is this about?" Sabian yelled. "Shut your damn mouths, we ask the damn questions, do you understand me?" The Asian guy who was in the restaurant said. Detective Hue Sun started squirming and moving around aggressively in the back seat. Then the other Asian guy who was sitting in the passenger seat bellowed. "Will you shut him the hell up and control him before I blow his fucking head off." Then he pulled out his gun and aimed it at Detective Hue Sun's head. "No, no, no, please don't please don't," Sabian begged as he fell over all his words. "Don't shoot, don't shoot." I shouted.

"Where are the secret files, we want them now assholes, do you understand me, or your friend the Detective is dead, he is fucking dead." Said the Asian guy with great force. Sabian looked puzzled and looked at me with a dumbfounded expression on his face.

"Secret files, what fucking secret files are you talking about, we don't know anything about any secret files." Sabian said as he looked at me. "What secret files, we don't know what you're talking about," I said while trying to sound convincing. Detective Hue Sun started moving around aggressively once again and the Asian guy in the passenger seat who had the gun, hit the Detective Hue Sun so hard in the side of his head; he started bleeding instantly.

"No, no, don't hurt him." I yelled. "Stop fucking playing with me, Mr. Vector we know you have the damn files, now hand them over dammit." Said the Asian guy who was driving the car. "How do you know my name?" I asked. "No more fucking games, now hand over the files now, or his ass is dead." The Asian guy with the gun said. "Mr. Vector, what secret files are they fucking talking about?" Sabian asked with a whisper, but I ignored him.

"I am going to count to ten and if you do not hand over the files or tell me where they are at, I swear, I am going to blow his fucking brains out, now!" Said the Asian guy with the gun. Suddenly, he began counting. Sabian and I slowly started moving backwards, and then I shouted. "We don't have any secret files." Before the count of ten we heard a loud pop. The gun went off. Detective Hue Sun head slumped down and blood was all over the back window. Sabian started shooting wildly and the Asian guys shot back at us.

Sabian managed to hit their radiator and front tire as we bailed into our car and quickly sped off. "Oh shit, oh shit, they killed the Detective." Sabian said when trying to talk while out of breath. "I know, now go, go, let's get to the hotel before they kill us." I said. "Who were those fucking guys, how did they know your name, and what damn secret files, are you hiding something from me Mr. Vector?" Sabian asked.

"It's a long story." I said. We made it to the hotel. Sabian parked in the back, so no one could see the car and I filled him in on everything. This was too much to deal with. We weren't ready for all this! Now it's inevitable, we must let the President know everything!

Chapter 10

The President Wouldn't Listen

{Ten}

That evening Sabian and I made it to the Presidents' Press Conference. It was hard getting in with all the security and news reporters, but Sabian's connection got us right in there. We sat and listened to the President of the United States discuss the impeachment trial he was going through.

"I know the Democrats are behind this, let me tell you they are wasting their time, I haven't done anything wrong, you see they are knick-picking, you'll see, you'll see, I have done nothing wrong, nothing." President Daniel T. Crump said. After several speeches, the President also talked about some of his Advisors being investigated by the FBI for espionage, but he stood firm and said these were all lies made by the Democrats. I took offense to what he was saying because me myself, I am a Democrat, but regardless of the differences of our parties, I knew I must tell him what's going on.

After the Press Conference was over, Sabian and the Presidents' Advisor got us connected with the President. We went and sat down in an office inside the White House. Marines guarded the door as we spoke. The Presidents Advisor named Dan Royce walked in with us.

"Mr. Dan Royce who do we have here, are they spies, or FBI or what?" The President said with an ugly smirk on his face. "No Sir, this is my good friend Sabian and his friend Mr. Vector, they are both world-wide known Scientist." Mr. Royce said.

"Scientist, huh, is that right, so why they are here, are they trying to get money or funding, because I don't have it, and no, I am not giving, now what is this all about?" He asked with a cocky attitude. I could tell right out the gate; he was a damn idiot.

"No, Mr. President, we aren't looking for funding, but we do have bad news." Said Sabian. "I've heard enough bad news, and I am going through an impeachment case as you can see that doesn't make any damn sense, no sense at all, so spit it out, what is this all about?" The President asked.

"Hello, Mr. President, I am the lead Scientist at Stanley F. Pharmaceuticals, we were sent over to China to assist in discovering a vaccine for a virus, we were sent to the Pandemica Compound in Wuhan, one of the most influential Compounds that engages in science and biology, as we became close to a cure, we found a Chinese man name Mr. Wu, was planning on infecting all of the world, including America with this virus like some type of chemical warfare." I said.

Sabian looked at the President to see what his response would be with his eyes widened. "Say what, no one is doing anything to us Americans, this can't be right, there certainly can't be any truth to this, who sent you here with this bullshit, was it the Democrats, is this another ploy of theirs to get me out of office?"

"It's true Mr. President, Mr. Wu took a virus and he amped it up by injecting the virus from a bat and infused them together and then he injected several people, now many people are dying in China, I mean they are dying at an alarming rate, if you don't believe us, then check it out for yourself." Said Sabian.

"Mr. Royce who are these people?" The Presidents asked once again. "Mr. President they are Scientists, please, just hear them out." Mr. Royce said.

"Mr. President, me and my team, came very close to a cure over in China, but we were interrupted by the corruption, now there is a man named Mr. Wu and he does have ties to America someway, he is now here and he's injecting people with this virus and if you don't believe us, turn on your TV and watch what's going on in China, I am sure you have connections and then look at what's now going on right here in America at our hospitals, it is now beginning, and we need to stop it now." I said.

The President slowly turned around and grabbed the remote off the table and turned on the flat screen TV behind him. He turned and saw all the deaths that were going on in China and he couldn't believe it. He changed the channel and saw how the America hospitals were starting to admit patients with some new kind of illness. He then, turned around and said, "China seems to have everything in control. If it hits here, we Americans will be able to handle it, besides; this virus might just come and go in a few weeks or so, no worries." He said. I couldn't believe what I was hearing.

"Mr. President, we must take this very serious, many people will die and maybe millions, we must act on this now, America will not be able to deal with this unless we're prepared." Sabian said. "Mr. President, please listen to them," Mr. Royce begged.

"Sir, there is a Doctor in China named Mathew Lee Su, he's also involved in finding a cure and in addition to that he has the virus, he warned the Chinese government on how contagious this virus is and instead of looking to find any evidence on this, they have guards outside his hospital room ready to take him to jail because of what he knows." I said while trying to convince him how urgent this was.

"If all of this is correct, what do you advise me to do Mr. Vector?" The President asked with sarcasm. "We may have to close the whole country down, which is similar to quarantining, meaning all non-essential businesses shut down and no one is allowed outside without a mask for at least thirty days."

"Are you out of your damn mind, do you know what you're asking, no, not under my administration, no way, that has never been done and never will, this virus will blow over, now enough talk of this." Said the President. "You're making a big mistake Mr. President." Sabian said. "Mr. Royce, show these Scientists out." The President said with emphasis. "But, Mr. President." Mr. Royce said with a sigh.

"Out, see them about their way." As we were getting ready to leave, the Vice President Michael Wince walked in and just stood by the President's desk. "Mr. President Sir, here's my card, we will be in touch soon, I'm sure of it," I said and sat my card on his desk.

"Come on Sabian, let's go." I said and we walked out behind Mr. Royce. Mr. Royce walked us out of the White House and we thanked him for everything he'd done to get us in there to talk to the President.

"Mr. Royce, we will be back, I promise you." I said, and we left. While sitting in the car, Sabian looked at me and he asked. "Why didn't you tell him about the secret files, the Asian guys who killed Mr. Hue Sun, and they tried to kill us, maybe he would have listened."

"He's an idiot, and he wouldn't listen to reason regardless, I think he has too much on his plate anyway, besides, most Americans don't want him in office, look at him and how he talks to people, he's an asshole. he only thinks of himself, and that's why he's going through this impeachment."

"I guess you're right, but so many people will fucking die if he doesn't listen, but do you really think closing the whole country is the only way to get ahead of this deadly virus?" "Honestly Sabian, a lot more than that needs to happen, but it's a start, don't you worry, Mr. President will call us soon, until then, we must get back home, and get into the labs and continue our work to find a cure." I said as we headed back to the hotel.

I got a phone call as we were headed back to the hotel. "Hello, hello, who is this?" "Mr. Vector is this you?" Mr. Lui Pand asked. "Mr. Lui Pand, how are you doing?" "I am doing as well as can be, but I have bad news, I know you are well aware of what is going on here with all these catastrophic deaths from the virus, but I thought I needed to share with you about Mathew Lee Su. He said.

"What happened to Mathew Lee Su, is he still sick?" "It is worse, he has died from the virus and it was very devastating." "Oh no, last I heard he was being accused of starting up some crazy lies about the virus." "Yes, our government accused him of evil things, but I guess now many people are calling him a hero, because he was only trying to warn our country of what is to come."

"What happened, what happened, what's going on?" Sabian asked as he was driving. "Mathew Lee Su has died from the virus; I'm talking to Mr. Lui Pand now." "Who's that Mr. Vector, who are you talking too?" Mr. Lui Pand asked. "That's Sabian, I'm with him now, and we're in D.C. leaving a meeting with the President of the United States." Suddenly, I heard complete silence. "Mr. Lui Pand are you there?" I asked a few times. Then I heard the phone hit the floor. I repeatedly called out Mr. Lui Pand's name.

"What's wrong Mr. Vector?" Sabian asked as he swerved near a sidewalk while driving. "Hold up, watch the road." I said as I called out to Mr. Lui Pand once more. Then I could hear Mr. Lui Pand arguing with someone. I yelled out again, but no answer. The arguing got louder and then I realized, I recognized the voice. It was Mr. Tan Saki, and as I called out to Mr. Lui Pand once more, I heard gunshots. I yelled and yelled and then the phone just went dead.

"Mr. Vector, what happened, what the fuck, happened?" Sabian asked. "I heard Mr. Lui Pand and Mr. Tan Saki arguing, then I heard what sounded like gunshots and then I heard nothing but silence." "Call back, keep calling back, I'm going to park the car in back of the hotel just in case those Asian guys are still after us."

"I'm trying, I have his number on speed dial but no answer, okay, park over in the corner, no, hold up, hold up, I see a black car with tinted windows near the entrance, take off, take off." I yelled out, before they could spot our car. "What about our fucking things?" Sabian asked. "What about our lives?" I yelled and Sabian pulled off quietly so we weren't noticed.

We drove around until we found another hotel on the other side of town. While there; I made reservations for us to fly back home and when I was finished, I turned on the news to see what was happening in the world. Sabian went and took a shower why I caught up on what was going on. It saddened me to see so many people were dying. New York seemed to be getting hit the hardest at this time. I really wish the damn President had listened to me.

Chapter 11

The President Finally Steps In

{Eleven}

Sabian and I flew back home and shortly after, we received a call from the President. Apparently after more and more deaths started occurring, he realized he needed our help. I was so angry, if the idiot had listened to us, all those Americans wouldn't have lost their lives. Now we had to come up with a remedy to contain this virus. Once again, we were back in D.C. at the White House. We sat and listened to another one of his rants at his Press Conference.

Apparently, Congress didn't have enough evidence to impeach him. He stood on the podium and gloated about it. In the back of my mind I was thinking, *"Is this even necessary, so many people are dying?"* That's just the humility in me. I just listened as he spoke.

"Congresswoman Peggy Spinelli knew she didn't have anything on me, this was just a ploy from the Democrats, you know they don't like me, I don't know why, but you know what, I don't like them either, they're mean people, moving on, we American's are now getting hit by a virus and this isn't just any virus, it's a China virus, yup a China virus." Mr. President Daniel T. Crump said. All I could do is put my hands over my face in shame.

"This virus is amongst us and it is spreading, places like New York, California and I think Louisiana are getting hit the hardest, they are the hot spots, now I am building a task force against this virus, well some call this a virus, but I call it a Pandemic, an ugly Pandemic, a scourge and it's going to take all of us Americans to do something we have never done before; and that is for non-essential businesses to close and everyone stay in your homes until further notice." He said.

The reporters had so many questions for him and I think he was overwhelmed because he kept making stupid comments. "Mr. President, how long will Americans have to have to stay inside their homes?" A reporter from CBN TV station asked. "Not long, not long at all, I believe this China virus will come and go, hopefully in about fifteen days or so, first it will be around us, and the next day it will disappear like it never happened." Mr. President said. "How can you be so sure?" A reporter from SBC TV station asked. Sabian looked at me and I looked at him and we just shook our heads. *Why is he giving all Americans false hope? Why is he commenting on information he knows nothing about?* I couldn't wait until this Press Conference was over.

After the Press Conference was over, we all got together in the Oval Office and I expressed my concerns to the President about how he was not speaking from a scientific view to the American people and he said, "What do you know, these are my people, they will listen to me, I'm a great leader, now tell me how can we slow down the spread of this virus?" I couldn't believe this asshole of a President.

"Until we find a vaccine, we may not be able to slow this virus down, we need to get all the information from China, and we need to find out how they're controlling it."

"I'll get Michael, our Vice President to get the information, didn't you mention a Doctor name Mathew something found a cure?" Mr. President asked. "No, Sir, I said he was involved in finding a cure." "Where is he now, can we get a hold of him?" The President asked. "Mr. President he is dead, the virus killed him, he warned China about how deadly this virus was and they were about to imprison him." I said.

Finally, Sabian spoke up after listening to the two of us converse with one another. "Mr. President, may I say something here?" "Sure, what is your name again?" Mr. President asked. "My name is Sabian, Sabian Daniels, Mr. President, well, first thing we need to do is stop all flights to and from China, now!" "Stop all flights, are you crazy?" Mr. President asked.

"Mr. President, he's right, as a matter of fact, we need to stop all incoming and departing international travel." I said. "This is absurd." Mr. President said. "People lives are dependent on it, Sir." Sabian said. Then the Vice President walked in the room. "What's going on Mr. President?" The Vice President asked. After we informed him, he began to make all the necessary phone calls.

"Mr. President, we may need to do more than just make people stay home, we may need to shut down all non-essential businesses in America, if we are to get some kind of control of this virus." I said. "Are you out of your mind, this is unprecedented." Mr. President said. He got up, and paced around the Oval office, and then he sighed.

"Sir, sir, Mr. President, are you hearing us, if not, just turn on your TV, and see for yourself what's occurring in our country right now." I said, and he did just that.

There were so many deaths starting to spread all over the world. Other countries were infected. New York's Governor was having a Press Conference, and he was saying people were dying daily by the hundreds. The hospitals weren't prepared for this volume, they needed respirators and bed space for many new patients. Soon, other Governors from other states also followed. After seeing all this, The President finally made the necessary calls to shut the entire country down; which was something that has never been done in our time?

The President hung up the phone and looked at me and Sabian and said. "How did this all start and who started it, I need to know, and I need to know now." I informed him about Mr. Wu and the Pandemica Compound. He sat there and quietly listened.

"This Mr. Wu is a dangerous man and he must be stopped, I'll notify the FBI about this monster, because a monster is who he is, no one, and I mean no one, will do this to America." Mr. President added. "Mr. President, Mr. Wu is here in America, and he's the one who is injecting our Americans as we speak, he's somewhere out there." I said.

"Mr. President there is something else we need to tell you, there are some Asian men here who may be working with Mr. Wu, and they killed a Detective we were working with, while trying to kill us at the same time." Sabian said. "What, I will let our Generals know what we are up against." Mr. President said and immediately Vice President

Michael Wince got on the phone and made the appropriate calls. While he did that, I advised the President about Mr. Lui Pand, Tan Saki and Mr. Lee.

"Now, this Pandemica Compound, is where all of this started at, well we need to get to Wuhan and destroy it, it sounds like a bad place, a bad place it is, let's get to work, now is there anyone else who we can get to build this task force, Mr. Vector, I want you in charge." Mr. President said.

I was about to speak, we heard gun fire coming from automatic weapons. We immediately hit the floor. As the President slowly put his head up to the window, his security was engaging in a gun fight with what appeared to be some Asian Terrorists. When it was all said and done many were killed, and the Asian Terrorists who were still alive, jumped in a white Ford van with tinted windows. Sparks hit the van as the shots from the Presidents' security guns bounced off the van. We were definitely in a Pandemic and a war at the same time.

Now this was apparent to the President, we were under attack. He then jumped into action after we all got up off the floor. "Michael, make sure we catch those assholes, call all the General and get all our fire power, we are at war with two enemies, one being invisible and the other is Chinese terrorist." The President said.

"Mr. President, I don't think the whole country of China is behind this, I just think it's some individuals." Sabian said. "I don't care, these are bad people, and they must be dealt with accordingly." The President said and I just shook my head.

"Michael, get a hold of that Doctor who was in charge of the Aids epidemic, what was her name?" Mr. President asked. "Dorothy Birch, Sir, I also called Dr. Baucci and General Flang, they will be a part of the task force along with Mr. Vector here, the American people lives are counting on it." Vice President Michael Wince said softly.

The President requested another Press Conference and we all stood with him. He knew what was next had never been done before. "I called this Press Conference today to tell the American people that we must shut down all non-essential jobs, all international travels and all trades for at least fourteen days." "Why, Mr. President, what's going on?" The reporter from CBN TV station asked. "This virus, is now taking over our health care and we must get control of it." Mr. President said.

"I thought you said this will blow over and go away, are you sure you are in control of this virus, Mr. President?" The reporter asked. "You are fake news and you know that, everything you say is fake, I never said that, I never said that, who are you working for, oh yea CBN, that's why your ratings are low, next." Mr. President rudely said.

Then there was a loud commotion amongst the reporters. Sabian and I looked at each other and we were disgusted on how the President acted. We were glad when this Press Conference was over. It was definitely a train wreck. Afterwards, Sabian and I got together with Dr, Baucci, Dorothy Birch and we informed them about our findings. The President sent us to a laboratory that was hidden so we could all do our research. We needed to find out as much as we could. It was a good thing Sabian and I were already ahead of the process because of what we witnessed in China.

By now the Pandemic had spread to one hundred and forty other countries. Americans were dying by thousands a day. We all felt helpless. As we were leaving the laboratory, Sabian walked over to me and whispered, "Our best bet is to spend our time on getting this damn cure, but it will take at least 18 months, Mr. Vector." "We don't have 18 months, we need to find a vaccine immediately, but we also need to find Mr. Wu, he must be stopped." I said and Sabian nodded his head up and down. Later that evening while meditating at a Quarters in the White House, I received a phone call from Chancie. She sounded very scared and agitated.

"Honey, what's going on, I see so many people dying on TV, what is the President going to do about this and when will you be home, the children and I don't feel safe?" "Calm down Chancie, we are trying to get this under control; I am not sure how long this will take, I'll ask the President to send for you and the children so you can be closer to me." "Can we fly to where you're at?" "I'm not sure it's safe right now, but I'll make sure you guys are secure and near me honey, please bear with me and oh, don't go anywhere, we are about to lockdown the country because this virus is deadly, so stay put until you hear otherwise."

"Okay, honey, we'll wait here until you send for us." "Thank you, Chancie, I love you and the kids, hopefully we'll get through this nightmare." "Be careful and we love you too, bye," She said as she hung up the phone. I then made the necessary steps to make sure my family would be safe. The President flew them to a nice secure place.

Meanwhile back in the Oval Office, we were summoned by the President for a meeting. Vice President Wince was there and he began to speak to us. "Mr. President, many of our health care workers are now overwhelmed, many states need our help, the Governors and the American people need our help badly, they don't have the necessary supplies which are needed, and I do believe if we don't get what they need, at least a million or two million will die."

"Is that the worst-case scenario, and if we get all the supplies they need, can we knock that number of deaths down to the one hundred thousand?" Mr. President asked. "With litigation Sir and if all the American people do their part with regards to staying inside for at least fourteen days, I believe so." Vice President Michael Wince said.

"Mr. President and Vice President Sir, I believe we will need more than fourteen days." Dorothy Birch said. "Well, right now we are going with fourteen, we can't afford to keep America closed down for that long, it will ruin our economy." Mr. President said,

"Mr. President what's more important, the economy or the lives of American people?" Asked Sabian. "Is that a trick question, who is this guy?" The President said with a sarcasm tone. "It's just a damn question, Mr. President." Sabian said. The President ignored Sabian. You could tell he was pissed off because his face turned pale.

"Mr. President, we will definitely need a little more time," I said. "You won't get it, fourteen days is all, now Michael make sure you get all the supplies to all hot spots especially New York City, they need it mostly." The President said.

"Mr. President, the reason why we need more time is because we must get over the curve and what I mean by that is our health care workers are getting overwhelmed by the number of daily cases and we can't keep up, we need more time so we can flatten the curve, so to say." Dorothy Birch said.

"Flatten the curve huh, let's see how this thing plays out and if we need more time, when it comes, I'll give it, but not a second before, and if anyone defy my commands, you will be fired, do I make myself clear, now Michael set up the Press Conference so I can announce our plans to the American people." The President said. "Okay will do, Mr. President." Vice President Michael Wince said, and he left the room.

"Mr. President, there's something else you need to know, there's a drug called Hydroxychloroquine which may be of some use, but it only seems to work on some patients, it might be of some use although it's not fully tested by the CDC." I said. "Okay, why didn't you tell me this before?" The President asked.

"Like I said, it hasn't been properly tested and it may harm more than help, but I do know one person it did help back in China." I said. "Okay, find this drug, we must get it tested and approved." The President said. "It may be dangerous Sir." Sabian said. "I don't care, let's find it and use it." Mr. President said. All I could do is nod my head. *Why is this man so pigheaded?*

Chapter 12

Quarantines Begin

{Twelve}

As we continued to converse in the Oval office, the President ordered the Armed Forces to head out to Wuhan and find the Pandemica Compound before he set out the plans for the total lockdown. Many soldiers were already near that area in China.

Then he sent Sabian and me to New York to find out as much as we could. We had to join the frontline workers and then report back to him. Dorothy and Doctor Baucci carried on with experiments as they looked over all the notes Sabian and I left for them. Right before quarantine, the President had another press conference. Sabian and I watched while sitting in a hotel in New York City. He ranted on and on.

"My fellow Americans, we have to go in quarantine this Friday, March 15th, this is unprecedented that our country must shutdown, but we trust that all of you will be taken care of afterwards, all non-essential jobs around the country must shutdown and they must shutdown now, this is serious and until we get to the bottom of this, everyone must stay inside." Mr. President said over and over.

Sabian and I got tired of listening to him. It was time for me to go to bed, I received a phone call from Mr. Lee. I hadn't heard from him for a while since we got him out of custody. "Mr. Vector, what is going on, so many people are dying, and do you still have the secret files with you?" "Yes, I still have them, but they aren't exactly with me, I put them up in a safe place."

"Do you know when you can get them for me?" "I'll get them to you as soon as I get back home, Sabian and I are here in New York on a mission for the President of the United States." "Okay Mr. Vector, which hotel are you staying at in New York?" He asked.

"Sabian what hotel is this?" I asked Sabian. "Who the hell is that?" Sabian whispered. "It's Mr. Lee," I whispered as I took the phone away from my mouth. "Oh, tell him we are at the Aloft Suites in downtown Manhattan." Sabian quietly said and then he laid down in the bed.

"We are in downtown at the Aloft Suites in Manhattan," I said. "Okay, well, let me know when you can get the secret files to me, Mr. Vector." *Damn, what's in those files and why does Mr. Lee want them so badly?* I thought to myself. We got off the phone and I looked over to where Sabian was lying down, and he was fast asleep, and I followed him as I laid down.

The next morning, we both woke up, and got ready for day one at the hospital. When we got there, it was overwhelming to see so many people going into the hospital. We were led through the back way so we good get fitted in proper PPE, by a Doctor named Forshaw Wilkinsburg, he was the head man in charge. We had to put on two long blue gowns, goggles, gloves, face shield and two pair of rubber gloves. It was hot wearing all of this stuff, but we had too for our own safety. Our jobs were pretty much to monitor all activity.

We entered the fourth floor where most of the patients were being treated. I have never in my life seen so many people sick at the same time. This hospital was out of control and dead bodies were being taken out right and left. They were trying to save as many as possible, but there wasn't enough equipment to save everyone.

Flatline sounds rang out throughout the halls. Doctors were literally running from room to room. Some patients were sitting in chairs in the hallway breathing through ventilators. So many people were coughing and sneezing. Every one of the Nurses were heavenly dressed in PPE and there were those who weren't. The ones who weren't; were getting sick and coughing. Another situation that startled us, was some Nurses wore torn plastic bags as gowns, because they were running out of PPE. This was chaos.

While we walked around, Sabian started taking notes regarding various issues that was going on and for everything that was needed. We followed Doctor Forshaw downstairs to the back of the hospital.

"Mr. Vector, Mr. Daniels this is sad and overwhelming, look at this." Mr. Forshaw said. All we could see is forklifts carrying what seemed to be wooden coffins with dead bodies in them. "What's in these boxes, are these dead bodies?" Sabian asked. "I'm afraid so, we don't have enough room here, we have to get these boxes made and by the end of the week, we'll run out and many of the bodies will be stored in freezer made trucks."

"Oh my God this is bad, what about funerals, how will the families identify their love ones?" I asked. "I'm sorry to say that most of them won't have a funeral and some of the families asked to have them cremated, but we can only do so much, just yesterday eight-hundred and ninety-six people died in one day, we need more space, where are we going to put all these people, I've already requested for more freezer trucks to arrive." Doctor Forshaw said in a saddened voice.

“This is worse than the two Civil and the Vietnam wars combined, you should see what’s going on in China and the rest of the damn world.” said Sabian.

“You both are Scientist, do you know where this started, was it really China who started this virus, are they the reason for this entire Pandemic?” Mr. Forshaw said as he directed the question to me. “I can tell you this, I don’t believe it was China, but individuals within China, bio-chemically constructed the virus for their own evil reasons and they will pay for it.” I said. Just watching all these bodies hauled off was horrendous, I swear. We walked around a little more and had extensive conversations with Doctor Forshaw.

After the day was over, we headed back to our hotel. When we got back to our room, Sabian sent over all of the information to the President by email. I sat on my bed in exhaustion. There were many feelings which went through me as I thought about all of the deaths. Thoughts of Shareen came across my mind and I started tearing up. All these deaths, this could have been prevented if the President had listened to us from the beginning. So many lives could have been saved.

Day two of visiting the hospital was a little more intense. Hundreds of people were in line to enter the emergency room. The line extended all around the way around the block. People were cursing and causing chaos out there. Fights broke out and the police had to arrest many. A man in line coughed and two Spanish guys beat him down to the ground and then they ran off before the police could apprehend them. About three people picked up the badly beaten man and walked him into the emergency area where two Doctors brought him into a room.

We couldn't believe this mess. America was starting to look just as worse as China. That day at least 786 people died in one day; including several other deaths in other hospitals in the area.

The last day was right before everyone would be quarantined for 14 days and it was a busy day. More and more people were dying. The loud noises of flatline sounds rang out. Some of the Nurses were crying because they couldn't save everyone. Tears even came to my eyes. We promised Doctor Forshaw we would get all the help he needs. I could see he was thankful, but I also could see the humility in him. He was in pain internally and I could see it written all over his face. It was hard for us to leave that day, but we had to go.

We made it back to our hotel room, packed our clothes in our duffle bags and went off to sleep. Before daybreak, I heard a noise out front. I nudged Sabian so he could wake up. "Sabian, I think someone's out there, listen." I quietly said. "Yes, I wonder who the hell it is, who's out there?" He asked as if he was scared. I kneeled by the window and I could see a white van and several Asian guys going to the checkout entrance.

“Oh shit, we got to go, get your bags Sabian.” “Go where, who is it?” “It’s those Asian guys from the White House, they found us.” “But how, how would they know where the hell we are?” “I don’t know, but let’s go out the back window.” “What about the rental, Mr. Vector?” “We have to leave it, come on now, let’s go.” I said as we grabbed our bags and jumped out of the back window.

I could hear the door kicked down as we ran out the back. I saw an Uber car drive by us. I yelled out, “Hey, hey, stop, we need a ride, we need a ride.” The Uber driver immediately stopped and he said, “Where are you going, come on get in.” “Hey son, what’s your name?” Asked Sabian. “Hi, I’m Tim Monetti, where are you going in a hurry this early?” Timothy asked. “Take us to the airport please, Timothy.” I said. “Okay come on let’s go.” Said Timothy. “How much are you charging?” Sabian asked. “The usual, don’t worry, I won’t charge you a lot, now let’s go.”

When we made it down the street, about four stop lights, I could see the white van driving fast. They got stopped at a light where a lot of cars made a right turn, and we eventually blended in with all the traffic. Luckily, we made it to the airport and got our tickets.

While we waited for our plane, we bought a few hats and a wig from one of the stores inside the airport. We went to the restroom and came out in our disguises. It was a good thing we did, because about five Asian guys were in the airport lurking. I immediately put the hat I bought on my head and put my head down and slid down next to a great big column inside the airport. While they were still looking for us, we got up and stood in the hanger as our plane came and announced for us to board. That was a closed encounter.

We made it back to D.C. and back to the White House, just in time for the Presidents' next press conference. "As you all know at midnight, we will go into a fourteen-day quarantine and we need all of Americans' cooperation, we're going to need everyone to stay inside to flatten the curve, that's right flatten the curve, isn't that what you said, right, Doctor Baucci?" The President asked as he looked at Doctor Baucci instead of the camera.

"Flatten the curve, what does that mean Mr. President?" A reporter from CNS TV station asked. "The virus is here and the virus is real, yes flatten the curve, look; we just got this information from these good people, they are incredible and they've done incredible work here, they are two great Scientists, Mr. Vector and Sabian Daniels, they are good people." The President said.

"Now with this quarantine, are we closing down the whole country?" The reporter from CBN TV station asked. "Yes, non-essential business only and it's never been done before, but to stop the virus it must be done"

"I thought you said the virus was temporary and it wouldn't stay no longer than fifteen days or so, you said it would disappear one day and go away, did you not Mr. President?" The reporter from CBN TV station asked in sarcasm. "Excuse me who are you?" The President asked. "I am David Wyatt from CBN News." Answered the reporter.

"Exactly what I thought, you report fake news like that other reporter, this is why your ratings are going down, you tell lies about me and the American people, be nice, be nice." The President said.

"I am only quoting what you said at the last press conference." The reporter said. "Go back and read what I said, I know what I said, you are fake news and I don't like you." The President said.

Then an Asian reporter stood up and she asked, "Mr. President how long have you known about this virus, shouldn't you have told the American people about this virus before so many people got infected?" "I knew, but I didn't know, anyway as soon as I knew, we started the procedures to stop all flights to China and internationally, we were early, if not more people would have died."

"That's not answering my question, Mr. President." Said the Female Asian reporter. "What's your name and who do you work for?" Asked the President. "I am Gi Gi Lee from CNS News, what does that have to do with anything?" Gi Gi asked. "You are fake news too, just what I thought, why don't you ask China." The President rudely said.

"Why don't you just answer the question?" Gi Gi asked. Sabian and I looked at each other in disbelief. Doctor Baucci tried to hide his face. “Look, when we found out, we jump on it, now next.” The President said. Gi Gi kept talking and interrupting the President. “You are rude, I answered your question now give someone else a chance.” Gi Gi kept talking while one of the other reporters tried to ask questions.

“I am done for today, no more questions, quarantine will start tonight, you can only go out to essential stores to purchase food and stores with toiletries, I am going to need everyone to stay at home and all non-essential businesses closed, that’s it for now.” The President said and he walked off the podium while reporters were still trying to ask questions. I knew we were in for one irrational ride. Especially since we were following a leader who was out of touch, he was only about himself and it was so obvious.

Chapter 13

The Days after Quarantine

{Thirteen}

Quarantine time was set for only fourteen days, but as soon as the President realized the results of the number of deaths, he had to order thirty more days. We told him from the beginning 14 days wasn't enough time and our health care and non-essentials workers were being destroyed. Many essential frontline workers got sick and some were overworked. Some were quitting their jobs and a head Nurse in Virginia committed suicide by hanging herself.

Finally, the President ordered thousands of ventilators that were needed for the hot spots and much needed PPE. New York City got most of their supplies, which was good because they were the hotspot, and they needed the most help. The hospital Navy ship docked in New York City to help with the overwhelming sick patients. There were no more boxes left for all the bodies that were laid to rest and they just placed a tag on their toe with their information. No funerals could be held at this time so many families didn't get to see their loved ones put to rest. It was atrocious. The President and reporters were going at it every chance they got. The President was saying awful things to the press and this wasn't making the situation any better. From state to state the virus was spreading and a massive number of Americans were dying. We had not seen anything like this in our time. But as I read and researched in China, this Pandemic had struck America in 1918, so I knew what we were up against.

As we got close to the quarantine lockdown to be lifted, Sabian and I were called into the Oval office by the President. "Mr. Vector, I am going to need your expertise in this little town in Montana called Choteau, they are in need of some guidance to keep the spread of the virus out of their state, can you and Sabian go there as soon as the quarantine is lifted?"

"Sure, how long will we be there, Mr. President?" I asked. "Just a week, we really need to help these people, they are good people and they are courageous, but they need our help." "We are on it now, Mr.

President, when do we leave?" Sabian asked. "Right now, we'll get the flight for you now, and thank you." The President said and just like that; we were on a flight to Montana.

When we landed in Montana, I looked down at my phone and I could see where I missed a phone call from Mr. Lee. I decided I would wait until we got our luggage before I called him back. We picked up our luggage and we started walking towards the car rental. I was looking all around, just to be aware of my surroundings. As we stood in line waiting for our car rental, Sabian turned and asked, "Mr. Vector do you still have those secret files and why haven't you told the President about them as of yet?" "Yes, and they are in a safe place, you know, I'm not sure who I can trust, I mean just look at our President, he's out of control, I don't think he should have them, I was told to give them to Mr. Lee."

"Do you know what's in those damn files?" "Sabian, I do not, but it seems like I'm not the only one who wants to find out." I said with force. Sabian immediately got quiet and turned to the lady at customer service and grab the keys for our rental. We drove to a small town and we got our hotel. While I was unpacking, I received another phone call from Mr. Lee.

"Hello, Mr. Lee, I see that I missed your call earlier." "Mr. Vector, yes I called to find out if there is any news, did you find a vaccine for the virus yet and is the President of the United States funding this?" "So far Mr. Lee, we're still working on a vaccine and the Government is backing everything." "I am glad they are; deaths are spiking and we are set to reach our peak of deaths by tomorrow." Mr. Lee stated.

"People are dying at an alarming rate, but the curve is different in different states, we're now in Montana, Sabian and me, we are just here to get the people of Choteau ready just in case the virus strikes this rural area with a population of nearly five thousand." "Oh, you are not in New York anymore, you are in Montana?" "That's correct and I got to tell you, there is a very cold and chilling feeling in the air, no one is outside, it's a stillness and calmness in the atmosphere, it's a crazy feeling, it's so quiet."

"Are they not on some kind of lockdown?" "Yes, but the virus hasn't really hit here yet, maybe four or five people, but I guess they were being cautious." "Okay, okay, so are you alone, who are you with, is Sabian still with you?" "Yes, Sabian and I are on this mission together."

"I must ask you; do you think you will ever come back to work for Stanley?" "I'm not sure at this time Mr. Lee, a lot has gone on with the spread of this virus and all, there will be a new normal for a while, but who knows."

"I hope everything goes back to normal, and yes there is one other thing, well perhaps two other things I need to ask you." "When are you guys coming back home and when are you bringing the secret-files?" Mr. Lee asked in a whispering tone. "Mr. Lee why are you whispering, anyway, to answer your questions, I'm not sure when we are set to come back home, because we're working side by side with the President of the United States and as far as the files, I have them in a safe place, I don't think now is a good time to discuss them, if you know what I mean." "I understand, you are on a mission, I was just curious, I want you to know you are doing an excellent job, you and Sabian, but can I tell you something else before we get off the phone?"

"What's that Mr. Lee?" "Your President is an idiot, an imbecile." "Yes, I know he is, but he is in charge." "Not really, but he is because he blames this all on China and now the Chinese Americans are getting hit with hate crimes and death threats." "I'm sorry to hear that, he is very careless with his mouth, I'll make sure I pass on the fact that Chines Americans are now getting targeted because of his words." "Be safe Mr. Vector and may the world rest in your hands, alright bye." Mr. Lee said as he instantly hung up the phone.

"Who was that Mr. Lee?" Asked Sabian. "How did you guess?" "All the questions he kept asking, said Sabian." "Well he sure talks a lot, damn, it's so quiet here, and where are all the people?" I asked as we walked toward the window. There wasn't any movement outside.

That night was an uncanny one because we kept hearing wild animals and they seemed so close to us. I guess the wild animals were getting adapted to not being people on the streets, they were coming out now. I was curious and I walked to the lobby to talk to the person running the hotel, who was a young woman and her name tag read Sandy.

"Excuse me, are those wild animal sounds I hear out there?"

"Yes, it is and I advise you to stay in, for some reason since the quarantine they come out at night and they've been known to attack people, I guess it's too quiet for them now." Said Sandy. "Or they are just hungry, uhm, do they come out during the day also?" "I have heard they do, and my advice to you be careful, hell I have to carry my gun to work every day now, that's all I can say Mr." What she said floored me, I gave a smirk and I went back to the room.

When I got back Sabian was snoring his ass off, but I couldn't sleep. I even thought I heard human screams and yelps. I wanted to hurry up and get the hell out of this strange town, but we had to help the people of Montana.

The next morning the ban was lifted in some of the states. Finally, the quarantine was over at least from our stand point. When I finished showering, I got a phone call from Mr. Royce and he gave me all the information I needed and he told me who I had to meet. I woke Sabian up and he got himself together while I texted Chancie to see how her and the children were holding up. She said they were doing well, but they just miss me. I let her know that I felt the same.

We arrived at a huge hospital in the middle of nowhere and help set everything up they needed that day and I gave them all the data about the virus to upload on their computers and servers. After we completed our mission, we got in the car and headed back towards the hotel, I asked Sabian to pull over to the side of the road; because I noticed in a far-off view, some mountain lions gathered around some kind of prey.

"Sabian look, look, do you see that?" I asked as Sabian stared in the same direction of the mountain lions. The more they tore and shredded whatever they were feasting on, it was evident it was of human remains. "You see that, I think it's a human body, look, that's an arm right there." I yelled out. Sabian slowly stepped out the car. "No, Sabian get your ass back in here." I shrieked. The mountain lions heard my yelp and they ran towards our car." "Get in, get in, pull off, now, now Sabian." I said as I was scares shitless. "Oh my God, oh my God, that was close Mr. Vector, did you see that fucking shit, they were eating a human body." Sabian said in a squeamish way.

"That was close, oh my God, that was close, now, let's get the hell out of here." I said. We drove through a nearby town and it was empty and quiet. I could tell the streets hadn't been occupied in a while because shrubs were growing through the cracks of the concrete. As we slowly drove through, we started seeing wildlife come out. Goats and their calves were following each other. As we drove around a curve, we spotted another wild cat, it looked like a cheetah or leopard or something. We watched it as if it jumped over a wall as if it was searching for food. Sabian spotted a lioness eating on remains, but all we could see was bloody bones.

"We must call the authority because these animals are clearly taking over." I said. "They're probably eating these fucking people." Said Sabian. "Let's get back to the hotel." I said. "Oh shit, damn, it's a bear." Sabian yelled out as he swerved. "You missed it, you missed it, go, go." I shouted out.

We made it to the hotel and I called the authorities and I contacted the nearest TV station and made sure they announce this news to all of the residents. "Please be careful coming out after the quarantine lockdown because the wild animals are out and they are taking over, they reported."

Now, everyone was aware of what was going on, but not everyone listened. That night it was more of the same except, this time Sabian and I were awakened by a cry of help from a woman and her son about twenty-five feet from the front entrance of the hotel. There were some coyotes moving in on them as they were trying to make their escape. Sabian and I grabbed whatever we could. I grabbed a mop and Sabian yanked the toaster off the counter in the lobby. We headed toward the entrance, but it was too late. The coyotes grab the boy's leg and they went ripping and tearing and we could hear his screams.

Sabian started yelling and swinging the toaster, but the coyotes wouldn't budge. A bigger coyote started heading for the woman and she was screaming. I yelled to Sabian, "Give me the rental car keys, give me the keys." Luckily, he had them in his pocket. I ran to the back of the hotel and I jumped in the rental car. I pulled around front and the coyotes were biting the woman and the boy on their arms and legs and they were bleeding pretty badly. I pressed my foot on the gas and floored the rental into the coyotes and they screeched loudly. Then they ran away. Sabian and I rushed the woman and her son inside.

We called for Paramedics to come. Her son kept going in and out of consciousness as he was bleeding heavily and the woman was just screaming in pain as she saw the huge gouge of flesh out of her leg. It was terrifying. Sabian ran into the laundry room and grabbed towels to stop some of their bleeding. It was blood all over the floor. About twenty minutes later the Paramedics and the police showed up.

As they were carried out and taken into the ambulance, I noticed an all-black car with tinted windows parked and turn its lights off. I assumed it was just someone watching from afar. Sabian and I cleaned up as much as we could, maintenance will have to finish the rest. We then provided the Officer all the information about what happened. He praised us for our heroism and reassured us the problem with the wild animals was going to be taken care of the following day.

I was exhausted and shaken up. I went back into the room and I stared at my hands as they were literally shaking, Then Sabian said he left the toaster near the door of the entrance, he had to go back down to see if it still worked and plug it back in the wall.

I waited for nearly ten minutes and Sabian didn't come back and I called his cell phone. I heard something ringing on Sabian's bed. I lifted up the sheets and it was his phone ringing. Something felt odd, I jumped up and headed downstairs to see if there were a problem. When I made it to the entrance, I couldn't believe my eyes. It was Mr. Wu and he had Sabian in a choke hold with a hand gun in his hand and he started screaming and yelling. "You didn't think I would find you did you, you son-of-a bitch, Mr. Vector, now where are the secret-files, give them to me, or I will kill this worthless American, now, hand them over dammit." He shouted and spit flew out of his mouth everywhere. Sabian started coughing and his face started turning blue.

You are killing him, let him go, he doesn't have the secret files, I do, please, you are going to kill him." Sabian tried to speak but he started choking. "Hand them over now, or I will inject him with a lethal dose." He said as he pulled out a syringe from his pocket.

"No, no, okay, I will get the secret files for you." "Now, get them now, I am not fucking joking with you, I will blow his fucking brains out now." Mr. Wu said. Suddenly, I heard a growling noise. Mr. Wu looked to his left and he immediately let Sabian go as he was attacked by a mountain lion. I grabbed Sabian and pulled him inside the hotel as he choked and coughed.

Mr. Wu tried to grab the door so he could get in. I pushed the sofa that was sitting in the lobby in front of the door to make sure he wasn't getting in. Another mountain lion showed up and they were just feasting on Mr. Wu's legs and arms. I heard his gun go off a few times, but not even his gun could keep them off. They ripped Mr. Wu to shreds and he screamed in agony.

"Sabian, are you alright, are you okay?" "Mr. Vector thank you, thank you." The next day the authorities showed up and they began shooting tranquilizers at all the wild animals. The only remains the police found from Mr. Wu was his hand and the gun. After this situation, I made a call to the airport so we could head back. When we were leaving, I looked to my right and I saw the syringe Mr. Wu had. I grabbed it and put in in my duffle bag. I knew I could use this to find out exactly what we are looking for when it comes to a vaccine.

"Mr. Vector, let's get out of here." Sabian said. "I agree Sabian, its's time to get back to the frontline." I said and we jumped into the rental car, which was slightly dented from running into the coyotes. When we landed back in D.C., we had our hands filled with more of the Presidents mess. *So many more people were dying. Will we ever get back to normal?*

Chapter 14

More people are dying

{Fourteen}

We made it back to the hotel in D.C. and we turned on the TV. The number of deaths had now quadrupled. The President was still in denial and at the same time he was trying to get the economy back going. But most of the Governors from each state was against doing so too early. Another hot spot started up in Detroit, Michigan and mostly the African American community were being affected. Once again, we had to be in the presence of another one of the Presidents disrespectful rants at his press conference.

"The virus, this scourge is almost gone, I mean not literally gone, but in my mind it's going and it's going fast, in fact we might have a vaccine or a medicine called Hydroxychloroquine that may slow up this virus, it's such an ugly thing, this scourge, maybe we should try this drug, what do you think Mr. Vector?" The President asked as he looked over at me. In my mind I was thinking, *"What the hell is wrong with this idiot."* Instead I just acted as if I didn't hear him.

"So, Mr. President, are you saying you have a cure already?" A reporter from CBN TV asked. "Ask Dorothy Birch, she is the expert here, ask her." The President said as Dorothy slowly walked up to the podium.

"Hello, this drug has not been proven yet, we don't know if it will work or not, but I have been informed it worked on some and others it hasn't been so affective." She said as she walked off the stage quietly. The President gave her a nasty look, but that didn't stop him from spewing out crazy shit. I couldn't believe he took the conversation he and I had and twisted the story all up just to benefit himself.

“Mr. President, the Governor of New York said they need more supplies, do you plan on sending them the materials they need?” The reporter from UGL TV station asked. “We sent the Governor of New York what they needed and more, they wanted ventilators we sent them ventilators, besides, we just ordered one hundred thousand more, who do you work for, what TV station?” The President asked.

“Then you will send more supplies if necessary, correct?” The reporter asked once more. “Who do you work for, I asked once, and I am asking you again.” Said the President. “I’m Tony Ginette and I work for UGL TV station.”

“Just what I thought you’re trash and the station you work for is fake news, that’s why I don’t like you, you deliver the American people fake news and I don’t like you; you are bad people, you know we are doing a wonderful job, don’t you?” The President asked. All I could do was shake my head and I was so glad when the press conference was over.

We all walked back into the Oval office and conversed on what was next. *What was the plan?* “Michael, I want you to make sure all the ventilators get to New York and make sure the state of Florida gets enough beds for their hospitals.” The President said to the Vice President. The Vice President got right on the phone and immediately started ordering everything that was needed.

"Mr. President don't forget to send the city of Detroit what they need also, from what I hear the number of deaths has spiked there as well." I said. "Mr. Vector, how do you know so much?" The president asked. "Because I conduct research, Sir." "Oh, you're a wise ass aren't you, anyway, I will make sure Michael gets on it, now tell me what happened on the mission I sent you on."

"You won't believe what happened Mr. President." Sabian said. "Did I ask you, now Mr. Vector what happened?" The President said with an arrogant tone. I explained how we helped the hospital in Montana get prepared and how we gave them the data they needed to prevent a massive spread in their town.

"We need to find that Mr. Wu guy who you told me about, that bad man, because he is a bad man, he needs to be stopped." Mr. President said. "Well Mr. President there's something else I need to tell you, we don't have to worry about Mr. Wu, because he was killed." "Yes, he's dead Sir." Sabian said. "I didn't ask you, am I talking to you?" The President asked. Sabian immediately held his tongue. *What is this idiot's problem*? I thought.

"He somehow followed us up to Montana, I don't know how he found us, but he attacked Sabian and in doing so, he was eaten by some wild mountain lions." I said. It took me about thirty minutes to explain to him as if I was talking to a 3rd grader. He finally got the picture. Shortly after our conversation, I pulled out the syringe and I explained to him what it was and that it might help us in our quest for a cure.

Then the President got a phone call and we sat and listened as he talked to a few Governors who said the deaths spiked again and it was said at least three thousand people are dying daily and it will probably last for a couple of months. When the President got off the phone he was even more pissed off.

"These damn Governors want me to do their job for them, if that's the way they are going to act then I will do their damn job, now Mr. Vector, you, Sabian, Dorothy, and Dr. Baucci go to the laboratory and see what you guys can come up with, we need a vaccine and we need one now." He insisted. "Sir, it's going to take at least two years to find a vaccine, there's testing involved and we need a live host." Dorothy said with a crackle sounding voice.

"I don't care, we do not have that kind of time, just find a vaccine, a cure, hell, I'll even take it myself, find it, we need it now." He yelled. Dorothy put her handover her mouth and she looked flabbergasted. We all knew the President was crazy plus an asshole, but he was our leader.

Right before we were about to leave, the President got another phone call. We listened for minutes at him rambling with whom it was. Then he hung up the phone and grabbed the remote control and turned on the flat screen TV.

China was going through a second wave of the virus and they had to close everything down for another seventy-six days. There were so many deaths and they were digging thousands of graves right next to each other on a hillside. I had never seen anything like this. Then the news switched to Italy and they were even worse off than America. Everyone was ordered to stay in lockdown and the Police were roaming the streets and making sure everyone did so.

Next was the UK. As of now, they only had a few cases, but now more cases were on the rise. The Prime Minister was working on staying ahead of the virus so he ordered they all stay on lockdown even with only a few cases. The entire world was affected by this virus. I couldn't believe all this started from our experiments in the Pandemica Compound. Mr. Wu unleashed this on all mankind and now everyone in the world is fighting for their lives.

The President turned off the TV and looked at me and Dorothy Birch and then he sighed before he spoke. "This virus is deadly and we need to know how it works, how contagious is it, how long does it lasts on surfaces, I see the nurses and doctors on the frontline wearing all the PPE, I wonder what can we do to keep other Americans from catching this virus." The President pondered.

"We'll get on the research aspect of it, but far as I know, if we all wear face masks or coverings, that may be a start to protect us all." I said. "I do agree with that also." Doctor Baucci said after barely speaking a word. “Oh, he talks.” Sabian said jokingly. “Of course, I talk, but no one was talking to me or asking my input.” Doctor Baucci said.

“Oh, Doctor Baucci, he’s a talker alight, so tell us what you think Doctor?” The President asked. “I think we should all wear masks when in the presence of a large group of people and we should social distance away from each other.” “Social distance, what’s that, I mean how do we accomplish that?” The President asked.

“Germs such as particles normally spread from your mouth and your nose; therefore, covering over the nose and mouth with masks will work until we find a vaccine, but this is only a temporary remedy.” Doctor Baucci said and we all just listened. Everything he said made perfect sense.

“I think that would work, we have to order about a million more masks, okay we can do that.” The President said.

“As far as the social distant part, we can keep everyone at least six feet apart and this will slow up the process a bit.” I said. “Anything we can do to stop this spread, we must get on it and get on it now, so what are you waiting for, get out of the Oval office and find that cure.” The President yelled as he pointed towards the door.

We left the Oval office and headed to a hidden laboratory deep under the White House. We all worked at our own individual stations. As I researched and thought about all the data, we came up with in the

Pandemica Compound more information started filling up in my mind and then all of a sudden, I was saddened. I thought about the last time I talked to Mr. Lui Pand. I was hoping he was still alive. I stepped out of the laboratory so I could call him but he never picked up. I walked back inside the laboratory and I kept on working.

We were all exhausted, but we stayed up late working. We congregated together with our ideas and then we would go right back to the drawing board. The process was very intense as we thought we had come so close, but then the genetic code would not match. We knew there was something missing in the equation, *but what?* I was so tired after hours and hours of research, I had to sleep. I went into one of the other labs and fell asleep. I was awakened by the ringing on my phone. When I went to answer it, the ringing stopped. The phone number came up private and I couldn't tell who was attempting to call me.

I immediately jumped up and went back into the laboratory where everyone was working, but no one was there. I guess they all got exhausted and left. There was much work ahead of us, but I was aware, while, we are still trying to find this cure, we must go back to China and destroy the Pandemica Compound where all this chaos started and my only wish is to hopefully be a part of its demise. This COVID virus has wiped millions of people off the face of the earth in just a few months. This Pandemic must come to an end!

Chapter 15

The end of Pandemica

{Fifteen}

A few months later after the President helped get all of the supplies for every state which was a hot spot, Congress also jumped in to help. Then the President ordered the Armed Forces to step in to aid with building more hospitals. The curve was flattening in some places, but in others were hit badly and it was moving in slow motion. We still hadn't found a cure and it seemed it would take us years to find one. I eventually got exhausted. One day I ask that the President to grant me a leave to go home for a few days and I would work on the cure there. After fighting him with words, I was allowed to go.

When I flew home, I was surprised to see my home had been shaken and destroyed. I was glad Chancie and the kids were somewhere safe. My mind was blown by all this, but all my thoughts were, I hope they didn't find my safe with the secret files in it.

I went straight to my safe while breathing heavily. It was hidden so well. I was so happy to see it hadn't been found. I looked all around before I opened it. I had to make sure no one was watching. I slowly opened the safe and to my surprise, the secret files were still there.

Then I thought to myself*, should I open them here?* The suspense got to me and I opened up the files. I was flabbergasted. All along Dr. Mathew Lee Su, had all the data for the cure. It was sitting in our laps all that time. I sat down slowly on a chair and tears fell down my face. So many lives could've been saved. I wonder why he didn't just tell me; *I wonder why?* I said over and over. I gathered a few items and immediately headed back to D.C.

I explained all my findings to the Task Force and the President. He then set up a press conference to let the world know that in months to a year; the vaccine would be available to everyone who is in need of it. He was eager to get the economy back moving. Although he brought good news, I knew the media and all the Americans weren't happy with all his efforts. His rude mouth and burning of bridges, hurt his so-called image. All along he tried to make this Pandemic about him and not the American people. As the Press conference began, we all were getting ready to hear what the press would say and they didn't hold back any punches.

"Hello fellow Americans, today I bring good news, we have found a cure, but here's the thing, we won't be able to get it out to all Americans until early January of 2021, we still have many tests to do, but as far I can see, is we did a good job, we could've had millions of deaths here in the United States; but instead we only have one hundred thousand, which is good in my eyes, we did a great job." The President said over and over.

"What do you mean we did a good job, people have still died and the last I saw the deaths were leaning over the one hundred thousand mark, are you that lost?" The reporter from CBN TV station asked.

"You are mean people, look if it weren't for me making things happen, we would've had far more deaths." Said the President with cockiness

"The American people don't care if you did a great job, we want some answers, if you had paid attention to this virus before and at least warned the American people, then we would've had a fighting chance, many lives could have been saved and you call that a good job, unbelievable." The reporter from UGL TV station shrieked out.

"Hey, hey, I didn't hesitate, when I heard of this virus, this scourge as you will, I call it a scourge, I immediately jumped to action, I didn't wait, I started the travel ban, no one can come from China or any other country, see this is what I mean about fake news, you are fake and you know you're fake and that's why your TV station has low ratings, I did not wait, I jumped to action." Said the President.

"You want us to praise you, we are not going to praise you, so many people have died and you lied, first you said this would blow over, but it hasn't, now you want us to believe there is now a cure." The reporter from SBC TV station said loudly.

"Oh boy, here we go again, I actually kept the number of deaths down, you should be thanking me, but instead you want to tell lies, next." The President said as he interrupted the reporter from CBN TV.

"You're a liar, we don't trust you, where is this vaccine you're talking about, we need it now." The reporter from UGL TV said piercingly.

"We have a vaccine, we will be able to get it out in a year, or maybe even before that, I am here to save our American people, nobody wants to save lives more than me, I made sure every state got what they needed plus we will be ready if there is another wave of this virus and we are sending our troops over to China and destroy the people and the place who manufactured this virus." Said the President aggressively. The press got so rough on the President, he instructed all of us off the podium and back inside the White House without giving the reporters any reasons.

We immediately went back to the Oval office and the President made the necessary steps to send troops to China to destroy the Pandemica Compound and anyone who was still manufacturing this virus. He made it clear no one would take over America and strike its people with a warfare as this virus did to destroy lives. In my eyes, it seemed as if the President had to prove a point to the American people.

"Mr. Vector and Sabian, you know this place, the Pandemica Compound very well, I want the two of you to lead the way with our troops, these people, these bad people must be stopped and because of them, people have died who could have possibly been alive today." Said the President. I swear the President is an idiot. After laughter on my part, Sabian and I agreed to go and lead the troops.

After a fourteen-hour flight to Wuhan China, we went into action. The President had a special unit of Marines with large guns, and extensive amount of ammo and lots of grenades and bombs.

One of the troops set a bomb at the entrance of the Pandemica Compound and within seconds a low boom was heard. He blew the front entrance clearly open and we walked in cautiously. As we creeped by the first laboratory, we observed someone working inside there.

"Who is it Mr. Vector, can you see?" Sabian whispered.

"I can't see who it is," I said quietly. After I said that two troopers went inside and all we heard was gun shots and yelling. Then a large body came through the door and it was Mr. Tan Saki. He had a bomb strapped to his waist and he looked at Sabian and I and screamed, "You."

We all ran for cover and in an instant the bomb around his waist detonated and body parts flew everywhere. The blast threw me down the hall and one of the troop's leg was injured, but he kept on the mission while limping. His pants leg was soaked with blood. I thought to myself, I need a gun. Then I asked the trooper to give me a gun and he did. I stuck the gun in my back where my belt held it and we proceeded.

The head Sergeant ordered one of the troopers to set bombs around the Pandemica Compound while we headed to the laboratory to where Mr. Wu created this hybrid virus called COVID 19.

Suddenly, the alarm in the Compound blasted loudly in our ears. Then a bomb went off and glass flew everywhere. Smoke filled the hallways and we couldn't see anything. All we heard was coughing. Somehow, Sabian and I were separated from the troops. Then we continued our way to the laboratory.

"Mr. Vector, do you still have that gun?" Sabian asked with a nervous tone. "Yes, come on follow me." I said. "I'm right behind you." As we walked down the hall we were coughing and spitting up. My eyes were burning as if I had been sprayed with pepper spray. I kept on rubbing my eyes as we came up on the laboratory. They were burning so bad I could hardly see. I saw a nearby water fountain and hurried to splash water in them and then I wiped them with my shirt. That stopped my eyes from stinging and burning so badly. I stumbled into the laboratory with my eyes squinted and I could barely see, then I called out to Sabian.

"Sabian, Sabian, where are you?" I asked as my vision came back clear. Then out of nowhere, I felt a blow to the head from a metal object and the pain followed. I started fighting for my dear life. I couldn't see who the person was because of the brown hoodie over their head.

We tussled from one end of the laboratory to the other while knocking over small bottles of what seemed to be the virus. We both fell on the floor and punched at one another. I struck him and he struck me. As I tried to get him off me, the gun in my back slid under a cabinet. I grabbed for it and suddenly, I felt something hot go across my thigh. I looked down and I was bleeding from the slash of a razor.

My adrenaline was flowing as we continued to fight until the attacker got on top of me, he punched and punched me until I almost fell unconscious. As he was trying to choke me, I saw the gun under the cabinet and I reached for it for dear life. He pushed down on my face with the palm of his hand and I got my fingertips on the gun.

I kept grabbling for it until finally, I was able to clinch it and I raised it to his side and shot two times. He stopped in a pause and leaned to the side. I hurried to push him off me. I stood over him while breathing heavily and fast. I leaned over to pull the hoodie off his head and to my surprise with was Mr. Lui Pand. His eyes widen and I watched him take his last breath. I was in shocked. *But why? Why would Mr. Lui Pand be a part of this? Was he a part of this, all along? I thought to myself.*

My thoughts were quickly interrupted as I felt a sharp knife pierce the skin of my upper back and I fell as the blade stayed in my back. It felt like a ton of bricks hit me. I looked up as I laid in agony and pain. "Sabian, why, why, why are you a part of this?" I asked as the shock of seeing my colleague turn on his own country with no explanation.

"Shut the fuck up Mr. Vector, you are such a trusting and stupid man, you and your idiot of a President, this isn't about me turning on my country, I want power and money, my account has a rather large deposit coming to it as we speak." Sabian said.

The pain in my upper back struck me like a bolt of lightning to a tree. I tried to sit up slowly as my gun lie near my side. Sabian couldn't see it.

"How did you think they always knew where the hell we were, I worked with the Chinese all along, just trying to get my hand on those secret files and thanks to you, I got all the data I needed, there will be more chemical warfare virus plaguing the world and I will never catch it, because I now have my hands on the virus." Sabian said in a diabolical voice and laughter.

"Sabian you will never get away with this, your country trusted you and you betrayed us, nothing good will come of this." "Shut the hell up, I already won." Sabian said as he charged me as to grab the knife out my back and stab me again. I pulled the trigger of my gun as I aimed in an angle to strike his abdomen. Then a gun shot rang out. I looked up and Sabian fell to the grown.

In came the Sergeant and the troops. They grabbed me and ordered me out because the bombs were about to go off. The Sergeant grabbed my arm and lifted me up, I heard Sabian grunt. He was still alive. I looked at the Sergeant and he nodded his head. I aimed my gun at Sabian's legs and I shot both of his legs and we ran out of the Pandemica Compound. I could still hear Sabian screaming and yelling don't leave him.

We got far enough away and the bombs went off loudly. We all laid on the ground as the bombs destroyed the Pandemica Compound.

I was so glad it was over. As we sat on the plane on that fourteen-hour flight, I couldn't believe what transpired. Why is Sabian and Mr.

Lui Pand would be a part of something so evil. I was lost in my thoughts. I sat quiet as I watched one of the troops medically treat the other from his leg bleeding. I could see he was still in pain, but I didn't say a word. I knew then the world would never be the same. We would have to live a new normal until the vaccine was fully tested and available the following year.

By fall there was an election and President Daniel T. Crump lost the election to Joseph Wadley. He was our new leader as we waited for 2021 to come in with new hopes of the cure and a new life. I am Alexander Vector, the sole survivor of a virus that almost wiped out all of humanity because it got in the hands of some evil people. This virus is now said to strike every one hundred years, I hope the next generation is ready because we sure wasn't ready for The Pandemic of 2020.

THE END!!!....

a novel by

Charles Lee Robinson Jr.

2020

COVID STRAND 19

PANDEMICA of 2020

The Earth Stood Still

A FICTIONAL STORY!

This story was made up from only theories and imagination!

Made in United States
Orlando, FL
09 August 2025

63701935R00095